# The Sussex Gold

The Sussex Gold

by

Robert Turley

AuthorHouse™
1663 Liberty Drive
Bloomington, IN 47403
www.authorhouse.com
Phone: 1-800-839-8640

© *2011 by Robert Turley. All rights reserved.*

No part of this book may be reproduced, stored in a retrieval system, or transmitted by any means without the written permission of the author.

First published by AuthorHouse   09/22/2011

ISBN: 978-1-4670-0072-7 (sc)
ISBN: 978-1-4670-0073-4 (hc)
ISBN: 978-1-4670-0074-1 (ebk)

Cover Design by Keith Dodd – Dodd Graphics Consultancy
keith@keefart.co.uk

Printed in the United States of America

Any people depicted in stock imagery provided by Thinkstock are models, and such images are being used for illustrative purposes only.
Certain stock imagery © Thinkstock.

This book is printed on acid-free paper.

Because of the dynamic nature of the Internet, any web addresses or links contained in this book may have changed since publication and may no longer be valid. The views expressed in this work are solely those of the author and do not necessarily reflect the views of the publisher, and the publisher hereby disclaims any responsibility for them.

Chapter 1 – Sir Francis Wheeler

The carriage, drawn by four powerful black horses, rattled through the entrance to Portsmouth Harbour, and made its way to the jetty, which was guarded by six marines, resplendent in their red tunics. Pulling hard on the reins, the coachman brought his horses to a halt a few yards from the nearest marine, who stepped forward and opened the coach door to enable its passenger to descend. A short thin man with long black flowing hair exited, and made his way towards the waiting guard of honour.

Francis Wheeler portrayed an air of authority. Some others of his exalted rank would have ignored the marines but he stopped and spoke with them for a few moments. Admiral Sir Francis Wheeler, an officer whose career had been largely spent in the service of King James II, was to join his flagship. *HMS Sussex* had been launched from Chatham just eight months earlier, in April 1693, and was the pride of the English Navy.

Waiting for him at the end of the jetty was a ship's longboat with six seamen to row it, and his faithful second-in-command, Captain Robert Smith. As soon as Francis Wheeler occupied his place on the boat, the sailors cast off, rowing with a smooth rhythm heading for the Sussex with its eighty guns and crew of over five hundred.

The bitterly cold wind whipped across the water, severely buffeting the longboat as it left the protection of the harbour. Pulling the collar of his naval coat tighter round his neck Admiral Wheeler turned to Captain Smith and said, "Have you ever seen such a wonderful spectacle?"

Captain Robert Smith replied, "No, Sir, I have never before seen such a sight."

The Admiral wasn't only referring to his flagship but to the large fleet, of forty warships and one hundred and sixty-six merchant ships, which was gathering off Portsmouth.

Francis Wheeler reached up for the side as the longboat lurched against the hull and the seamen tossed their oars. Clambering up the hemp rope ladder, he climbed up to the upper-deck. Once on board the flagship the Admiral gave his instructions, "Captain prepare the ship, and fleet to sail for the Mediterranean. I'll go to my cabin for some refreshment, as I have travelled far and covered many dusty miles."

The admiral received his orders directly from King William III, who had replaced James II some years before. James II had lost the throne because of his inability to work with Parliament. His alliance with Catholic France and his arrest of Archbishop Sancroft, as well as six other Bishops, his failure to proclaim the Catholic Faith prohibited, made him an enemy of Parliament. Parliament appealed to William of Orange urging him to save England from a Catholic take-over. William gathered his forces and landed in England in November 1688. This so called Glorious Revolution resulted in the abdication of James II and his exile in France.

Although Francis Wheeler served the new king, he secretly hoped and prayed for James II's return to the throne.

"Batten down the hatches! Prepare to sail!" a voice yelled.

"Stand by to weigh anchor! Lively, you scum!" the mate shouted.

The Admiral settled into the comfort of his cabin, he could hear the sound of feet running on the upper-deck as men rushed to their allocated tasks. The helmsman grabbed the spokes of the wheel; men climbed the rigging to lower the sails, and gradually the ship came alive. As the heavy canvas sails filled with the power of the wind, the ship lurched forward and headed towards its fate.

Standing by the cabin stern windows, the Admiral slit open the sealed envelope, which contained his secret orders. These revealed that somewhere in the bowels of his ship, iron chests packed with nine tonnes of gold were stored. On behalf of William III, and amid utmost secrecy, Admiral Wheeler was to bribe the Duke of Savoy with the gold to keep him in the War with France, and allow the Grand Alliance to attack Louis XIV through his weakly defended southern border.

Francis Wheeler could not believe his luck when he realised what had been entrusted to him. *Could he convince Victor Amadeus, the Duke of Savoy not to use the funds as his orders indicated, but to use them instead to help return his beloved, deposed monarch to the throne?*

* * *

Almost six months had elapsed since he had last seen Arabella, his loving and devoted wife, who had supported him through thick and thin. He desperately missed his children too, especially little Anna-Sophia. This self imposed separation, from a normal family life, was one of the necessary sacrifices he had to make in order to fulfil his lifelong ambition to command a naval warship.

Democritus once said, *"Happiness resides not in possessions and not in gold, the feeling of happiness dwells in the soul."* Francis Wheeler now experienced this feeling as his thoughts drifted back to his childhood. He remembered the many times his father, Sir Charles Wheeler, told him stories of famous sea battles and of the Ships-of-the—Line which had taken part. His father had a natural gift for storytelling and recounted them so vividly that they had a profound effect on his young son. Even when he grew to maturity he often remembered the tales of naval Commanders, who had carved out their place in history with their battle successes and many deeds of valour.

Francis was extremely proud of his father and of his accomplishments. The tall, aristocratic figure had represented Cambridge University in the Long Parliament and had served as Governor of the Leeward Islands. Although Charles led a very busy and active life he still found time for his youngest son. Francis remembered the many hours his father had devoted to skilfully, and lovingly, building a model warship to give him for his tenth birthday. Little did he know then that he would spend over sixteen years of his life serving the Royal Navy? His father's gift became a treasured possession. Francis always took it with him on any sea voyage, and this posting was no exception. As he glanced at it now, where it held pride of place in his private cabin, he wondered if his father would have been satisfied with his achievements, if he had still been alive.

His naval career, as an officer, started with his appointment as second-lieutenant aboard *HMS Rupert*. Subsequent promotions soon followed. He commanded six different ships before arriving at his final command on board *HMS Sussex*, an eighty gun Third Rate Ship-of-the-Line.

Louis XIV was the most powerful monarch in Europe; but although he had expanded his realm the "Sun King" remained unsatisfied. His aggressive actions in extending his gains in order to stabilise and strengthen France's frontiers led to the War of the Reunions, and several years later to the War of the Grand Alliance. During this later war Francis commanded the ninety gun, Second Rate Ship-of-the-Line, *HMS Albermarle* and fought in the Battle of Beachy Head and the Battle of Barfleur.

Although the Battle of Beachy Head was the greatest French tactical naval victory over their English and Dutch opponents during the war, Francis was very proud of his brave men who had fought so valiantly. He remembered the courage of men like, Charles Ackley, Adam Crosier, Philip Samuels and Jim Seton. Jim had lost a leg and Charles was blinded when a French ship in the line of battle fired a broadside. The cannons of these men of war ships were accurate only at short ranges, but as the ships sailed closer and closer towards each other the cannon fire became effective. Francis Wheeler had seen many men killed or horribly maimed because of the destructive effect of the fire power from a battery of cannons.

The action at Barfleur was necessary when a French fleet was seeking to cover an invasion of England by a French army to restore James II to the throne. The French fleet was intercepted by the Anglo-Dutch fleet which included *HMS Albemarle*. Francis Wheeler found himself in an unenviable position. He wanted James II restored to the throne but knew that he could not be a traitor to his country and therefore had to engage the enemy.

His battle campaigns were numerous but his mind seemed to dwell on the failures rather than the successes. He remembered when he had led a fleet to attack French possessions in the Caribbean and North America. The attack on Martinique ended in failure when large numbers of the troops involved became sick. He floated the idea of an attack on Quebec, but insufficient troops could be found, and an assault on Newfoundland was similarly considered but rejected after the defences were found to be too great to overcome.

Chapter 2 – Cadiz

Richard Greene hated life on board ship and detested the confined and stark conditions. He could not get used to sleeping in a hammock slung between the deck beams on the gundeck. Food was disgusting, beef had been stored in casks for many years, and the ships biscuits were full of maggots. Sailing was not in his blood, he never had any ambition to join the Navy. The Press Gang had forced him against his will and deprived him of his liberty. The only thing that kept him from going mad was the small book of love poems that his wife Hanna had written for him. Managing to keep it in his possession, ever since his involuntary recruitment into the Royal Navy, he read it at every opportunity.

He had been in love with Hanna Martindale ever since he first met her. She had long beautiful red hair and blue eyes. Her freckled face gave her a fresh youthful image. He could never get her out of his mind and wondered if he would ever get back to Stepney to be with her again. He missed her so much.

Richard had finished his duties in the forecastle but as he came onto the gundeck he spotted John Crumwell rummaging through his belongings. John Crumwell was a bully and was always looking for trouble. It was rumoured that he had beaten a man to death just because he had accidently spilt a jug of beer over him in a crowded tavern. It was to escape being brought to trial by the Justice of the Peace that he ran away to sea.

"Put that book down!" Richard shouted angrily as he saw what John Crumwell was holding.

"Make me if you can. Which little whore gave you this?"

"Give it to me or I will break every bone in your body," retorted Richard as he made a grab to snatch his beloved book of poetry from the bully.

John Crumwell stepped back out of Richard's reach causing him to stumble and fall smashing his face onto the deck. "From your loving Hanna to my darling Richard," John taunted Richard as he lay spread-eagled on the deck by reading out the inscription Hanna had written.

As he started to push himself up Richard spotted one of the square wooden plates that was used at meal times. He grabbed it and threw it unerringly at John Crumwell's face and shouted "My wife isn't a whore."

The plate hit Crumwell hard on the bridge of his nose causing him to drop the book. Uttering a loud inarticulate cry of pain he viciously kicked out, catching Richard under the chin, and knocking him unconscious.

"That'll teach you. I'll make you pay dearly for attacking me," he then bent down and picked up the book of poems from where it had fallen on the gundeck and threw it out of a gunport. He saw it land on the crest of a small wave where it was overrun by some whitecaps and disappeared from view.

John Crumwell was just about to kick defenceless Richard hard in the ribs, but was stopped by the presence of Petty Officer John Loder, who had heard the commotion and had come to see what was going on. As Richard lay unconscious John Crumwell related his version of events which seriously departed from the truth.

"We'll let the Captain decide who started the fight." Turning to some seamen who were returning from their duties the Petty Officer ordered them to lock the two fighters in the hold overnight.

"Clang, clang, clang, clang, clang, clang" Six bells had sounded signalling the start of most of the crews day. The boatswain's mates blew their boatswain's whistles and called "All hands ahoy." This was soon followed by, "Up all hammocks ahoy."

If Seamen were slow to respond to this command, their hammocks were cut down with them still inside. As it was now seven o'clock in the morning, John Loder brought the escort party to fetch the two troublemakers. They were unceremoniously frogmarched and brought before the Admiral. Disciplinary hearings were always heard early in the morning for any punishment meted out would be administered at eleven o' clock, in front of the whole ships company.

Sir Francis Wheeler was not a cruel man but he knew that strict discipline had to be maintained at all times to keep rough and unruly crews under control. "These men were fighting. One of them nearly had his nose broken and the other was knocked unconscious, Sir," the Petty Officer informed the Admiral.

"What have you both got to say for yourselves," the Admiral asked.

John Crumwell spoke up first, "He accused me of stealing his book of poems but I never touched any book. I have never seen him with any poetry book."

"That's a lie," Richard retorted. "You knew I had such a book as I was always reading it every chance I got,"

"He nearly broke my nose just for the fun of it," Crumwell continued.

"You're a liar; you called my wife a whore. You were asking for trouble and had no right taking something which didn't belong to you." Richard said.

The Admiral listened to the two seamen with their different interpretations as to what had happened but he couldn't distinguish the true facts. "As there were no witnesses as to how the fight started and I don't know which one of you is telling the truth I have no alternative but to punish both of you. Fighting on board a war ship is a serious offence and therefore I sentence both of you to be flogged. You will both receive twenty-four lashes and then perhaps you will learn a lesson. Take them away Petty Officer."

The ship's crew had been ordered to assemble so that they could witness the punishment being delivered. The ship's surgeon was also in attendance. The two offenders were stripped to the waist and both were tied to a grating on the deck. The boatswain's mates removed their Cat o' nine tails, from the protective baize bags, and started to administer the punishment.

"I'll get you for this," John Crumwell mouthed as he felt the lash rip into his bared back.

Richard knew that he had made an enemy and would always need to be on his guard. His thoughts were soon interrupted as the boatswain's lash descended, and crisscrossed his back setting his skin on fire. He wanted to cry out in agony but was determined to show that he wasn't a coward and could take his punishment in silence.

"Aaaagggghhhh," again the lash fell on his lacerated back but Richard forced back another stab of pain.

*　*　*

A moderate breeze was blowing, filling the billowing canvas and driving *HMS Sussex* forward at a steady six knots. Admiral Wheeler strolled onto the Quarterdeck during the afternoon watch. The main deck was a hive of activity. He could see some deck hands scrubbing the deck. The ships carpenters were making repairs to defective timbers. Bosun's Mates were blowing their whistles to get attention and then passing orders through the ship. He heard the Bosun shout "Away aloft," sending some of the best hands high up into the rigging, climbing hand over fist, to make adjustments to the sails. Sir Francis knew that this was one of the most dangerous jobs onboard, especially in poor weather. A fall from high up in the rigging usually meant death or serious injuries. The Admiral was glad that he did not have to do this. A few seamen were slaking their thirst by drinking from the Scuttlebutt. Everything was as it should be.

"When will we reach Cadiz?" Francis Wheeler asked his second-in-command.

"We've made good time, and if this weather holds we will reach our destination the day after tomorrow."

The Admiral moved out of earshot of the helmsman and signalled for Captain Robert Smith to follow him. "What do you know about the Duke of Savoy?

"I know that he is one of our allies helping us fight against King Louis XIV of France, but that really is about the extent of my knowledge," The second-in-charge replied.

"His father died about nineteen years ago, and as he was the only child he became the Duke of Savoy. Being only nine years old his dominating mother, Marie Jeanne of Savoy, acted as Regent. Although he is married he is very fond of the ladies, and has had several mistresses. Under his mother's regency, Savoy was closely linked to and heavily dependent on France, but Victor Amadeus II changed all that when he broke this link. You are right when you say they are one of our allies. Geographically, Savoy is in an ideal position to allow a second front to be opened against France in the South."

"Why did you ask me what I knew about the Duke?"

"I'll speak to you further about this when we are in the privacy of my cabin. In the meantime I'll let you get on with running the ship." The Admiral replied.

*   *   *

With the advantage of a following sea *HMS Sussex* and the convoy reached Cadiz half a day earlier than expected. Francis Wheeler was still in his bunk when he heard a frenzied knock on his cabin door. "We're here Sir, We're here in Cadiz." William Batchford was the Admiral's cabin boy. Although he was only fourteen years of age, he was quite mature and dependable but a little excitable. He tried so hard to please the Admiral in everything he did and always had a smile on his face; no request seemed too onerous for him. William had seen both the inner and outer harbours filling up with the fleet, of merchant and naval ships, and he didn't want his Admiral to miss the excitement.

"Thank you, William. Please don't shout so loud I will be out shortly," the Admiral replied as he struggled out of his bunk.

Despite all his years at sea Francis Wheeler had never been to Cadiz Harbour before. He remembered however, that over a hundred years earlier Sir Francis Drake had sailed into Cadiz, and destroyed a large number of Spanish Ships that were gathering for the invasion of England. This was a more peaceful and joyful occasion and Francis Wheeler was pleased that his ships commanders would not have to call battle stations.

The first part of his mission had been a success. All the ships in his fleet had made it to Cadiz. They would spend some time replenishing their supplies then they would reorganise. Once this was accomplished the fleet would break into smaller groups to make their way to various destinations in the Mediterranean.

Before going on deck Sir Francis called his cabin boy, "I will be having a guest for dinner this evening. Will you lay another place at my table and make the necessary preparations?"

"Aye, aye, Sir," young William Batchford answered without question.

"Before you start your preparations will you take my respects to Captain Robert Smith and inform him of my dinner invitation and ask him to join me at eight o'clock this evening?"

Chapter 3 – I'm with you

Captain Robert Smith pulled up the collar of his greatcoat for protection against the chill of the night air as he stepped out onto the deck. The sky was grey and heavily overcast, but this would not stop his enjoyment of his routine evening stroll on the ship's quarterdeck. The wind was blowing steady and strong. He could feel its power as it bowled the ship along with the foaming seas beneath her bow. The creaking of the rigging and the groaning from the timbers filled his ears. His nostrils caught the tangy smell of the sea and he could taste salt in the air. As he looked down onto the sea, he saw the reflection of the moon. *This is a good place to be*, he thought.

Following Britain's conquest of Jamaica in 1655, rum had gradually replaced beer and brandy as the sailor's drink of choice. Some members of the crew would save up their rum ration for several days, and then drink them all at once. Due to the subsequent illness and disciplinary problems, Robert Smith had ordered that the rum be mixed with water, therefore diluting its effects. Robert Smith knew that the rum ration, to signal the end of the working day, would be issued shortly, but he would fare much better than this. As he had been invited to join the Admiral for dinner, he knew that he would be offered some fine wine to accompany his meal.

As he walked towards the bow, he saw Edward Asplin coming towards him. "Good Evening, First Mate."

"Aye, it is that, Cap'n."

Edward Asplin had served under Robert Smith before and owed the Captain a large debt of gratitude, for he had saved his life. Edward was born in Thame Village, Oxfordshire. He was six feet tall, weighing one hundred and eighty five pounds. He didn't have an ounce of fat on him and was very physically powerful. When drunk his bad and uncontrollable temper frequently got him involved in fights. His nose had been broken on more than one occasion turning his otherwise handsome face, with the piercing blue eyes, into an object of ugliness.

Some years earlier, Edward had got involved in a bare knuckle fight with a fellow seaman following a heavy drinking session in a Chatham Tavern. As the fight progressed, Edward was gaining the upper hand until three friends of his opponent joined in the melee. Edward didn't stand a chance against the four of them, and they gave him the severest beating of his life. He realised that they intended to kill him as he lay on the ground trying to protect his head from the kicks that were raining onto his body. From the pain in his side, he knew that at least one of his ribs was broken. He was choking on his own blood and, as he tried to cough to clear it, another crushing blow landed.

"Let's knife him and finish him off," one of the four assailants snapped.

"Stab him in the neck," another shouted.

Edward was absolutely powerless to do anything to defend himself. The brutality of the thrashing he had received was sapping his will to live. He steeled himself for the killing blow.

"Drop that knife and leave that man alone!"

This strong and authoritative command startled the attackers but, instead of heeding it, they turned ominously to meet the new threat. At first they just saw the one person in a strange uniform "We're not frightened of you. Go away or you'll meet the same fate as your friend here."

Captain Robert Smith advanced one more step and then stopped. As he halted, he was joined by a group from his crew who were returning to their ship. "Do as I say or I won't be responsible for the actions of my men when they take revenge for what you have done to one of their friends."

The gang of four, realising that they were outnumbered, turned and ran as fast as they could, leaving Edward in a very serious and life threatening position.

It took a long time but eventually Edward recovered and hoped that one day he would be able to repay the captain for his timely intervention.

The wind was getting stronger; buffeting Robert and forcing him to grab his cocked hat before it was blown off. Steeling his muscles to help him keep his balance, he continued along the quarterdeck. During this short respite from his duties, he was able to let his mind wander to more personal matters. When they reached Gibraltar, he would be able to spend a short time with his beloved Mary. The thought of her laughing green eyes and tempting smile made him hungry for her.

Mary had been born in Gibraltar and had lived all of her twenty five years there. She had met Robert Smith when serving him in the tavern where she worked. Despite the fact that she met many young and eligible men she had immediately fallen in love with him. He too became infatuated with her. He was twelve years older than her but he was determined not to let this be a barrier to their relationship. When he was discharged from the Navy he had promised to take her back to Gillingham in Kent, where he owned a small house.

When Robert Smith was granted command of his first ship his father had given him a beautiful and expensive repousee precision watch. He was very proud of this watch which had been manufactured by George Graham from Cumberland. The skill and craftsmanship which had enabled the case to be decorated with the image of Diana, the Huntress with her dogs, never ceased to amaze him. On checking the time he was surprised to see that he had only ten minutes to get to his Admiral's cabin where he was expected for dinner. *I must get a move on. It won't do to upset the Admiral by being late.*

* * *

"Thank you, William," the captain said to the Admiral's cabin boy as he took his hat and greatcoat from him.

"I'll inform the Admiral you've arrived," the cabin boy said.

While he waited to be ushered into the presence of Sir Francis Wheeler he wondered what would be on the menu. The principle source of protein on board ship was meat—pork and beef dried and salted accompanied by dried peas. As his mind began to fantasise about the forthcoming dinner menu he was disturbed when summoned by the cabin boy.

"The Admiral is ready for you now, Sir."

"Come in Robert, come in. I'm glad to see that you are punctual for we have a special treat tonight, and I wouldn't want to see it spoiled. Young William has managed to catch two fresh fish which cook has prepared for us. The cook has been hoarding some fine quality cheese which we are also going to partake of. Sit at the table and we will enjoy our dinner and then I have something to discuss with you."

"Thank you, Sir. It is sometime since I have had the opportunity to eat fresh fish and I am sure that it will bring me much pleasure."

The dinner was excellent. The red wine flowed freely and the meal was complete when the Admiral poured two glasses of vintage Port. The port had an intense colour with a subtle and fruity aroma. It was the best Port that Captain Robert Smith had ever tasted.

"Have another glass of this wonderful Port and then we'll get down to the proper business of the evening," the Admiral said.

The atmosphere in the cabin was suddenly changed. One minute it was very relaxed and good-humoured but now it became more sombre and intense. The sparkle in the eyes of the Admiral, which had been there all evening, was now replaced with a cold hard stare; locking onto Robert Smith and seeming to drill down to his very soul. Robert Smith found it impossible to drag his eyes away realising that something more dramatic was about to happen.

"Are you a supporter of James II or William III?" the unexpected blunt question from Francis Wheeler hit Robert like a thunderbolt from the blue.

"What do you mean? William III is our King and I am in his service," a somewhat surprised and shocked Robert Smith replied.

"You know what I mean. There's a large number of people who thought that it was wrong for Parliament to contrive for him to be deposed, and would do anything for him to be reinstated on the throne. Don't worry about revealing your true feelings, for whatever is said in this cabin tonight will remain between us, and no one else will ever know."

"I have told you Sir, I serve King William."

"I see that you don't fully trust me even although we have served together for many years, and have survived numerous terrible situations. To show that I trust you, I will tell you a secret that if it became common knowledge it could finish my career. I would do anything to have James II back in his rightful place. I have always had a feeling that you shared the same desire, although we have never expressed our views to one another."

Robert Smith was astonished by what he had just heard. "I never suspected that you had any such wish. I do trust you implicitly, Sir; and I would do practically anything for you. I don't know what made you realise that I too want James II back on the throne."

"My orders instruct me to deliver a large volume of Gold to the Duke of Savoy as a bribe, to keep him in the war with France. This mission has been surrounded with such a veil of secrecy that not even the Duke of Savoy is aware of the plan," Sir Francis Wheeler continued.

"Why do you need me? Robert Smith queried.

"I need someone that I can rely on to help me conceive a plan that would ensure that the Duke of Savoy withdraws his forces from the battlefield and returns them to their barracks. Or perhaps it would be better to persuade him to join forces with Louise XIV? If we can manage this

William III may be discredited and lose the authority of Parliament making it easier for James II to be restored."

"I'm sorry, Sir, but I have to say that this is a preposterous and foolhardy ambition and I can't see that it would work. If it failed and it was discovered that we were behind such a plan, we would be hung for treason."

Sir Francis became angry because Robert, although voicing earlier support for him, didn't immediately agree with the principles of the plan. "I know this plan is at the embryo stage but I am sure that we can make it work if we are determined enough. Are you with me or not?"

The silence that followed the Admirals outburst was stifling. Robert Smith's brain was a hive of activity as he tried to decide what he should do. "I'm with you," he whispered, in such a low voice that it was incoherent.

"What did you say?" snapped Sir Francis Wheeler.

"I'm with you."

Chapter 4 – Let's get down to business

What have I let myself in for? Robert Smith mused, as he made his way to his cabin. *Can the Admiral really believe that his plan could be achieved?* Fear of the possibility of the hangman's noose caused him to have an involuntary shiver, and violent shudder. The Admiral had always impressed Robert, for the way in which he was meticulous with the planning of the various missions they had been involved in, but the proposal to trick the Duke of Savoy just seemed reckless. Sir Francis Wheeler had proved himself to be a winner, achieving much by not shying away from dangerous and seemingly impossible situations. *I have always trusted the Admiral, so why should I change now?* These conflicting thoughts seized his mind, as he decided to take a detour and made his way on deck. He needed some fresh air to clear his head, and he hoped it would also help to nullify the effects of the more than several glasses of Port he had consumed. Half an hour later the remedy took effect; his internal turmoil became much calmer. Returning to the sanctuary of his cabin he undressed to his underwear, and collapsed onto his bunk. Consigning his doubts to the furthest recesses of his mind, he was soon fast asleep.

Time passed very quickly whilst in Cadiz Harbour. The weeks seemed to merge into one another, as Robert carried out his duties in ensuring that the fleet was restocked. He also played an important role in organising the small groups of ships that were to travel to various separate destinations. The Admiral had left him in charge, for he had business to attend to in Cadiz and would be gone for two weeks.

"While I am away, don't forget to give some thought to our plan," the Admiral directed. "When we sail from Cadiz, and make our way to Gibraltar, we can share our thoughts to come up with a workable solution."

"Yes Sir," acknowledged Robert.

Several days after Francis Wheeler had left the ship, Robert decided to take a break from his duties to go and explore Cadiz. It was a beautiful sunny warm day, and ideal conditions for exploring the oldest city in Europe. Almost entirely surrounded by water, the city appears isolated. It stands on a peninsula jutting out into the bay, dramatically defining the surrounding landscape. He knew that the Phoenicians, Carthaginians, and Romans had all settled there at one point over the years. Cadiz had a reputation of being very relaxed and easy-going. Even at night, people felt safe walking around the city.

Robert spent some hours meandering along the narrow, cobbled streets, which opened out onto pretty little squares. Eventually he discovered the old central quarter which he thought was the most beautiful part of the city. By the time he reached the central quarter he had worked up quite a thirst. It didn't take him long to spot the small tavern, sandwiched between a bread shop and a cobblers. The smell of freshly baked bread permeated the air. Upturned wine barrels, serving as tables, were placed just outside the narrow entrance to the tavern. He lengthened his stride and quickened his pace in order to quench his thirst as soon as possible.

"One large beer and a sherry," he ordered from the wizened old man who was serving behind the filthy, stained wood of the bar. Robert handed over the equivalent of two English pennies in payment, and took his drinks outside. Most of the wine barrel tables were occupied except for one that was in deep shadow. He would have preferred to sup his drinks while enjoying the heat of the sun, but it was better to sit in the shade than go back inside the tavern, which had a poor standard of cleanliness. It was only after he had downed his beer that he noticed the three men who occupied a table quite close to his.

At first glance it appeared as if the three men were locals enjoying a beer and catching up on the local gossip. One of the men was dressed in a Catholic Priest's cassock-style shirt. He appeared to be the oldest of the three men and had the most to say. The Priest's companions were as different as chalk and cheese in their physical appearance. The one with the scar on his left cheek was very thin and weedy looking. The last member of the group was very plump and had a ruddy complexion. As Robert had no knowledge of the Spanish language, he didn't have a clue about what was being said. However as the Priest was very agitated he had an inkling that they must be discussing something important.

Robert gradually felt that something out of the ordinary was happening. There were large glasses of beer in front of the three men, but they showed no interest in drinking them. As far as Robert was concerned that in itself was a crime. Beer was for drinking and should not be wasted. Usually there would be a lot of laughter and loud banter from such a group, but they were keeping their voices low and the conversation seemed to be quite intense, as they huddled close together.

Robert was careful not to show any interest in them, as he slowly sipped his sherry, but his ears pricked up as he surprisingly heard one of the men utter an oath in French. This caused the Priest to jabber a staccato of Spanish in an angry response. By this time he had finished his two drinks, but being intrigued about what was going on he went and purchased two more. When he returned he found the three men still in deep conversation. *Did I hear correctly? Was that really French that I heard? Why was the Priest so agitated? The alliance is at war with France so why would a Frenchman be in Cadiz?* He had no answer to those questions and they continued to puzzle him, as he started on his second beer.

This beer is really good, he thought, as he emptied the last drop from the glass. He didn't get this opportunity very often. He was enjoying the experience of being on dry land, away from the hustle and bustle of life on board a third rate ship-of-the-line. Suddenly his whole body stiffened, as he realised that the same man had lapsed into French again. He received a bigger shock this time for the man mentioned the Sussex by name. *What was going on?*

Spies! The word hit him like a hammer blow. *Could it be possible that Louise XIV had sent his spies this far from Paris? What am I going to do about this?* The three men stood up and moved away from the table.

After shaking hands each of them moved off on a different direction. Robert felt powerless. If he had some of his crew with him each of the three could have been followed, but on his own he could do nothing. He could only return to the ship and tighten the security that surrounded the *Sussex*.

There were only three days left until the Admiral returned, and then they would make sail for Gibraltar. During this time nothing untoward happened, and by the time Sir Francis Wheeler came on board Robert decided not to mention what he had witnessed.

* * *

"Good morning, Admiral." Robert was much happier now that Sir Francis was back. He could pass responsibility for the fleet back to him.

"I see that you have done a good job in my absence. I understand that everything is in order, all ships have been restocked and any necessary repairs have been carried out."

"Yes, everything has gone well. All the ships that were to sail for various destinations have all been despatched. We are just left with the ships that are to sail with us to Gibraltar." Robert informed with a feeling of self satisfaction knowing that he had pleased his commanding officer.

"Arrange for all ships' Captains to come on board tomorrow morning to receive their orders, and we'll inform them when we need to depart."

* * *

There was a great deal of commotion and excitement, amongst the crew of *HMS Sussex*, when the various Captains came on board to meet their Admiral. Everyone had arrived in good time for they all knew that their Admiral was a stickler for punctuality. No one wanted to be on the receiving end of his anger should they be late. It didn't take long to issue the necessary orders and notify them that they would make sail the following morning. Each Captain had also been instructed to use this last day to ensure that his ship was thoroughly cleaned and in a sea worthy condition. As soon as the Admiral had finished he informed the Captains to make no delay in getting back to their various commands, for there was a great deal to be done.

"Now that all the Captains have returned to their ships to make their final preparations, would you care to join me in a glass of Port?" The Admiral questioned.

"Yes, Sir, I would appreciate that very much," there was a small smile present on Robert's face as he responded.

"I would like to propose a toast," Robert announced as he raised his glass of Ruby Red Port, "To the success of our mission."

"To the success of our mission," the Admiral responded.

"Was your sojourn in Cadiz, fruitful?" asked Robert.

"Yes, it was. It had been arranged for me to meet with Viscount Galway, England's envoy extraordinary to the Duke of Savoy. I had no option but to do this in order to keep the pretence that I was still following the plan of the Lords of the Admiralty. I didn't want them to get suspicious before we are ready with our own plan." Sir Francis said.

"Why is the Duke of Savoy helping us?" Robert asked.

"England was prepared to recognise Savoy as a sovereign state and agreed to return Casale and Pinerolo to his control. Both of these strategic locations are in North-Western Italy. This was a very different policy to that of Louis XIV who had embarked on a policy of overt military intimidation. This policy convinced the Duke of Savoy that he had to stand up to French aggression."

"Do you still believe we will be able to convince the Duke of Savoy to leave the Alliance and help restore James II to the English throne?" Robert questioned.

"Yes," came the curt reply. "I know that representatives of Louis XIV have offered Victor Amadeus a large bribe to abandon the allies. I am convinced that we can persuade him to accept this bribe, and also take the large sum of gold which we carry on this ship."

Chapter 5 – The Storm

Poseidon, the god of the sea, was relied upon by sailors for a safe voyage on the sea. Sometimes horses were drowned in his honour. He was a moody divinity and his temperament could sometimes result in violence. When he was in a good mood, he created new lands in the water and a calm sea. When he was in a bad mood he would strike the ground with a trident and cause earthquakes, ship wrecks, and drownings.

Sir Francis Wheeler had made a study of Greek Mythology and knew of Poseidon. He struggled against the increasing power of the wind, and the erratic movement of the ship, as it was tossed about in the turbulent waves. *This must have been what it was like when Poseidon was in a bad mood.* Within a very short time the strong easterly wind reached gale force strength. The violent levanter that originated from the Alboran Channel was now playing havoc with the fleet.

"Tack into the wind and try to tuck back behind Gibraltar," Sir Francis ordered.

"You heard what the Admiral said. Get a move on." the tough and grizzled Bo'sun snapped to his coxswain, as the ship battled the storm.

Although Sir Francis was in overall command of the fleet, he would not normally take direct control of his flagship. This would be the responsibility of his second-in-command. He saw it as his duty however, to maintain a visible presence in such difficult situations. He had discovered over the years that this gave the crew a greater degree of motivation, especially when they were under such a vicious attack by the elements.

There didn't seem to be any pattern or rhythm to the sweeping of the decks by the great waves, which slammed down on the full one hundred and fifty seven feet length of the *Sussex*. Anything not securely fastened or tied down was turned into a weapon of destruction. The power of the body of water propelled it along the deck, as if fired from a cannon. There was no way the Admiral could have foreseen such devastation being vented on his ship. When in Cadiz everything seemed to be going well. He had been confident that, with the help of his second-in command, he could be instrumental in helping James II replace that upstart William III. Everything had now changed.

The first mate was struggling through the waves breaking on deck, when suddenly he was savagely crushed down onto the hatch, which covered the hold. The huge wave hit him before he had a chance to secure himself to the jackline. The howling wind prevented anyone from hearing his cry for help. He was powerless. He had spent half his lifetime at sea and had never experienced a storm as horrifying as this. The hard physical life, of a matelot, had caused him to develop a muscular frame. Even his great strength however, could not prevent the fast moving body of water playing with him, as if he were a child's doll. As it swept him from the hatch, his head cracked against a stanchion with such force that he was knocked unconscious. Then he was gone. As the wave retreated over the side, the first mate was taken with it. There was no hope for him. The ferocious waters, aggravated by the powerful winds, cradled him to his resting place in Davy Jones' Locker.

"Robert, I'm really anxious about the extreme degree of roll and pitch of the ship. If it gets any worse we could be swamped and easily capsized," Sir Francis said, as he tried to keep himself upright. It was only a small wave that poured over him, but it was powerful enough to nearly sweep him off his feet. His heavy coat provided insufficient protection, and he was drenched to the skin.

Robert suddenly grabbed the arm of Sir Francis, and at the same time pointed aloft. "What is that hanging from the ratlines? Is it a man?" Although only a few paces away, from Sir Francis, he had to shout as loud as he could to make himself heard above the noise of the storm.

"Nobody could climb up there in this weather. If it is a man he must have been there for some time." Sir Francis responded.

"Yes, I am sure it is. One of his legs appears to have been snagged in a rope rung of the ladder. I'm sure he has broken his neck from the way his head is lolling about."

The main mast had been weakened by the constant battering it had received. It had been designed to withstand the force of storm winds, but this levanter was exceptionally fierce, abruptly the entire mast with its spars and yards and cordage coming crashing down on the larboard side.

"Aaaagggghhhh," exclaimed Sir Francis, as a turnbuckle, which the wind had ripped free from its position, slammed into the side of his head. He collapsed immediately. Robert rushed to him thinking that he had been killed. His condition looked serious. He had sustained a large, deep, and jagged cut to his head. A heavy stream of blood was pouring out, but Robert was relieved that the force of the blow had not killed him.

"He is still alive!" Robert exclaimed to two nearby seamen. "Take him to his cabin, get him out of these soaking wet clothes and into a dry nightshirt, then fetch the Ships Surgeon to him."

Shortly after Sir Francis was taken to his cabin, Robert decided to get below in order to check the damage. He also wanted to see if there were any leaks. *HMS Sussex* was a typical third-rate ship-of-the-line, having just two gun decks to house its eighty-guns of various weights of shot. Robert was aware that senior officers in the admiralty had voiced concerns about the inherent instability of eighty-gun ships with only two decks. He knew that there was much debate about the possibility of adding a third deck to new ships of this armament. *Would the Sussex be able to cope better with this storm if it had three decks?* he thought as he fought his way down to the gun decks as the ship continued to plunge into the heavy sea.

Making his way along the first gun deck, Robert spotted that a number of gun ports were still open. He was shocked to find this, for although the crew had done everything in their power to secure the heavy cannons, and to lock away any items that could cause injuries with the severe movement of the ship. *Why leave an opening for the sea to pour in? What were the men thinking about? How could they be so stupid?* He didn't have time to voice these thoughts, but simply gave orders for the gun ports to be closed, before moving to the lower gun deck. This order never got actioned.

The raging tempest was too powerful and water poured unrelentingly through the open gun ports. Large waves crashed down, snapping the remaining masts bringing canvas, timber, and rigging onto the deck. Anything not fastened to the deck washed overboard. The ship sank half a mile to the ocean floor.

Admiral Wheeler's dead body, clad in a nightshirt, was found on the eastern shore of the Rock of Gibraltar; two days after the sinking, a surviving ship of the fleet discovered the only two survivors. The rest of the five-hundred members of the crew drowned. Twelve other ships of the fleet also sank with a total of twelve hundred casualties. This tragedy would remain one of the worst disasters in the history of the Royal Navy.

The secret funds never reached the Duke of Savoy. As the gold went to its watery grave so did the secret of how it would have been used. The desire of Sir Francis Wheeler, to help his beloved James II was never realised. A year later the Duke of Savoy accepted an offer from the French and changed sides. His defection brought the Nine Years War to an end in stalemate with the Treaty of Ryswick in 1697. William III remained as King of England, and Louis XIV ceased to offer much in the way of assistance to James II who died of a brain haemorrhage in 1701.

The gold would remain locked in the hold of the sunken *HMS Sussex* forever, or would it?

Chapter 6 – The Project

"Hi, Gran, are you home," Bill called as he let himself into his Grandmother's luxurious, and very spacious, bungalow in Four Oaks Park.

"Yes, dear, I'm in the kitchen."

He should have known better. His Gran loved to bake and her oatmeal cookies were to die for. If she wasn't in the garden, she was in the kitchen. He dropped his single large red suitcase in the hallway. The red suitcase accompanied Bill on every trip or journey. He reckoned it saved him a lot of time at airports, for being easily identifiable it could be retrieved quickly from the baggage reclaim area. Making his way to the kitchen, he said, "It's good to see you again, Gran, you're looking well."

Ever since Bill's parents died in a horrific car crash on the M6 motorway, his Gran had looked after him. Peter and Mary Wyman were only thirty four years old when the large, out of control, articulated Volvo truck ploughed into their Volkswagen Polo. They didn't stand a chance and were killed outright. It was lucky that Bill was not with them when the accident happened, for he had been on a school organised holiday in Italy. Although his Gran was a war widow, she didn't hesitate to take him into her home and brought him up, as if he were her own son.

Because her husband had died during the Second World War, Elizabeth Wyman needed to hold down a full time job, as she couldn't survive on a War Widow's Pension. She had been employed as an Accountant for a large furniture manufacturer. Bill regretted that he had never met his Grandfather, but because his Grandmother told him many stories about her beloved Gary, he always felt a closeness with him.

Gary Wyman had been a Royal Marine Commando serving in the 1st Special Services Brigade. He took part in the initial assault phase of Operation Overlord. During this allied invasion of Normandy the objective was to seize the bridges of the River Orne and the Caen Canal. Gary never even made it to Sword Beach, the code name for one of the five main landing beaches. He was killed, as he jumped from the landing craft, when a German Panzer Tank shell exploded in front of him.

Bill was always amazed by how his Grandmother's facial skin was wrinkle free and very soft, helping her to appear much younger than she was. She was very petite, being only four feet three inches tall and very slim. She possessed a very strong and determined personality however, which helped her to cope with bringing up a young boy on her own.

"I looked up my Horoscope just before you arrived, Bill," she said. "What a load of rubbish. As you know my star sign is Leo, and do you know what it said? *Financial gains can be made through wise investments. You'll get to your destination just as quickly. Your boss won't be too thrilled if you leave things unfinished.* I am retired and haven't worked for years. The Astrologer certainly got it wrong."

"I definitely don't believe in Astrology either. You have to make your own destiny in this world," Bill replied.

"I was really pleased to get your telephone call asking to stay a few days. You don't need to ask, I always have a spare room for you. It's only three months since you were last here so I must admit I wasn't expecting you just yet," she said.

"I know, Gran, but I am going to be tied up with a major project and may not be able to visit you for some time."

"What sort of project will you be involved in this time," she asked. Elizabeth Wyman always wanted to know more about his work. She never failed to show an interest in whatever he did; although she often wondered how he could afford the affluent lifestyle he led. Bill's Grandmother knew that he received a good salary, but she often felt that there were things he never told her about.

"As you know, Gran, I work for the Archaeological Review Group. We give advice to the Government and carry out projects on its behalf." He didn't tell her that sometimes he was able to misuse the privileges of his position to make personal gain. "Seven years ago a 17th Century document was discovered, but it has lain undisturbed in our archives until now. It was a wax-sealed sheet of vellum from a French spy in Livorno, Italy, which had been sent to Louis XIV. It tells of a secret mission involving Admiral Sir Francis Wheeler, his ship *HMS Sussex*, and a fortune in gold coins. The gold was locked in a series of iron-clad chests stowed in the cavernous hold, and destined for the Duke of Savoy in north-western Italy. However, the *Sussex* was caught in a severe storm, and sank somewhere near Gibraltar before the gold could be delivered. As far as we know the vast wealth is still onboard. I've been asked to research this, and provide an archaeological analysis for the Ministry of Defence."

Bill Wyman had a cold personality and had a low regard for members of the human race in general. The only exception was his Grandmother whom he loved very much. She had been there for him when he contracted the polio disease, when he was eighteen years of age. He would never forget what she did to help and support him. Although surviving the disease his left arm was badly affected. It was shorter than his right by three inches. Although the Neurologists had done everything in their power to mitigate the effect of this horrible disease, he only had sixty percent of the strength of his right arm, as the muscles in his left arm were severely withered.

Despite his disability, he had graduated from the University of Birmingham with a BA (Hons) Marine and Natural History Degree. His time at the University was not a happy one. A large number of his fellow male students seemed to have girlfriends, but he was unable to attract a girl mainly due to his useless withered arm. He was often made fun of by the girls and became rather frustrated. He remembered that he had a crush on a particular girl, but Julie would have nothing to do with him. It was her that christened him with the ghastly nickname *"Shorty,"* in reference to the length of his left arm.

"Gran, after tea, do you want to come for a spin in my new car?" Bill asked. He had always admired fast cars and recently had purchased a Jaguar XKR. It came with a 5.0 litre supercharged engine, as standard, but he had arranged to have a speed pack fitted to it. This increased the maximum speed to two hundred and fifty kilometres per hour. It was a beautiful and luxurious mean machine. He had chosen Kyanite Blue for its colour. The mineral Kyanite is reputed to bring tranquillity and calm. Bill found that when he was behind the driving wheel of this powerful car, he felt good.

"Yes, dear, I would like that very much. It will make a change from going on a bus. I wish that I had learned to drive when I was a young girl, but it's too late for me now," she replied.

The next few days passed very quickly, and before he knew it he was back in his London based office starting to cope with the project in hand. He was staggered to discover that the current value of the submerged gold coin could be as much as two point six billion pounds. This large figure was based on the fact that the estimated melt value was approximately one hundred million dollars. From experience, it had been found that similar gold coins sold for as much as thirty to fifty times their melt value. *This could be the richest shipwreck ever discovered.*

Bill knew that this was going to be a very complicated business. Even before contemplating the technical resources that would be required there would need to be some sort of agreement made with the different countries involved. There were no regulations governing archaeological practices in international waters. There had been many attempts to make such agreements but because of disputes between developing countries and important maritime nations, they failed to give the measures the force of law.

A crooked smile formed at his lips, as he realised the potential of his task. *There must be an opportunity to siphon off some of this wealth for me. The Duke of Savoy's loss could be my gain.*

Chapter 7 – I want a share of the Gold

Davy Alexander felt on top of the world, as he arrived at his office in the Ministry of Defence. He had just returned from visiting the members of the British Forces, who were serving with the forty three-nation NATO International Security Assistance Force (ISAF), based in Afghanistan. In his absence his office had been refurbished. It was with much pleasure that he eased his slim six foot frame into his new comfy executive style, medium back, black leather chair. He leaned back to test the posture support, a feature he needed to relieve any discomfort caused by his painful back problem. It was perfect. Before getting involved with the duties of the day, reports to read, reports to write, interviews and meetings, he took the opportunity to admire his surroundings.

His new furniture had been purchased from a company that had fulfilled commissions for King George VI and Queen Elizabeth. He admired the crown cut natural American Black Walnut desk, at which he now sat. Pride of place however, went to the barrel shaped solid edged board room table, made from the same wood as his desk. The matching workwall, incorporating concealed lighting, was also of a high quality. *At last I have an office worthy of my position, as Minister of Defence.*

In Afghanistan he had spent most of the time with the 4th Mechanized Brigade, the lead formation of the British Forces. He had been updated on some of the negative issues that were still causing problems. This included being informed about the soldier who had refused to join his unit. He didn't want to be sent to Afghanistan, for he believed it was "wrong in principle" for the British Forces to be involved. Conversely, there were many positive improvements that showed much progress was being achieved.

The security situation was a top priority for the Government, but his involvement extended to other areas, such as trying to improve working relations with the Afghan Government, tackling corruption, and building up the rule of law. None of these things were easy but Davy got a lot of satisfaction from trying to make things better.

Davy Alexander was proud of his achievements, both in the Trade Union Movement and now for the Government. He knew that he couldn't emulate the unique career of James Callaghan who had held the four great posts of Chancellor of the Exchequer, Home Secretary, Foreign Secretary and Prime Minister. None the less he was grateful for the opportunity to make his mark as a good Minister of Defence.

"Good morning, Minister. Sorry to disturb you, but I have brought you a cup of tea." Sarah, his personal assistant always brought him some tea when she arrived at the office. She had been personal assistant to three previous Defence Ministers and had proved to be very reliable and knowledgeable on many issues. He trusted her completely.

"Sarah, I am meeting with Bill Wyman, from the Archaeological Review Group, this afternoon, can you please bring me the report regarding HMS Sussex, so that I can get prepared."

* * *

After the usual niceties the Minister of Defence said, "Right gentlemen, as chairman of this group, I suggest that we get down to business. Earlier today I read the 17th Century Document that Louis IV's spy sent to him, so I am fairly well up to speed. Bill, can you start the meeting?"

Gathered round the boardroom table, in addition to the Minister of Defence and Bill Wyman, were Joshua Campbell, Parliamentary Under-Secretary of State and Minister for International Security Strategy, together with Sir Dennis White KCB, the Permanent Under-Secretary of State. Bill had brought Gillian Young with him. Gillian had been his assistant for a number of years, and was an expert in Treasure Hunting.

"As you know Sir, HMS *Sussex* was sunk with great loss of life, and an absolute fortune in gold coin locked in its hold. This happened in sixteen hundred and ninety four, but the wreck has largely been forgotten about until the discovery of the package written by the French Spy in Livorno."

"Yes, I am aware of the details. I know that the sea robbed us of our national wealth. For the best interest of the British taxpayers, I want it back." The Minister realised that he would also gain a lot of personal kudos and recognition if this could be achieved.

"There are a number of Archaeological Groups who have expressed concern regarding the preservation of the integrity of the site, where the Sussex lies. In fact some have gone so far as to say that they would prefer that this wreck had never been found. Such people seem to forget how much good can be done with such a vast sum of money," Bill said. He didn't mention that if some of the cache could be diverted to him, then he too could gain a lot of benefit

"Recovery of the gold will need meticulous preparation. We will also require the services of a company who has the right sort of technical resource. Getting the gold to the surface from a depth of some two thousand five hundred feet will be dangerous and time consuming." Sir Dennis commented.

"I know of a company who can handle it. Once you give us the go ahead, Minister, I will get in touch with them. I will also arrange for Gillian to work with the company, they will find her knowledge invaluable," Bill said.

"That's fine, but I also want Sir Dennis seconded to the project. He will have overall responsibility for security as we need to ensure this project has a top secret classification," Davy said.

"But Minister . . . ." Bill tried to put up a challenge to this for he didn't want anyone, who had direct access to the Minister, to be so closely involved in the project.

"There are no buts about it, Bill; this is how it is going to happen."

Joshua Campbell wanted to know more about the company the Government was being asked to enter into partnership with. "What is the name of the exploration company you have in mind, Bill? Have they a good track record? Where are they based? What sort of costs do you think are involved in this project?"

"I'll give you a full report once Gillian has had her initial meeting with the Chairman of the Company. Basically however, the company, AB Salvage, is based in Greenock, Scotland, and to my knowledge they have successfully found and salvaged over three hundred wrecks. I really don't know what the total investment will be but I would estimate that the minimum costs would be in the region of twenty five million pounds."

"That is a great deal of money," Sir Dennis said.

"If we succeed with this, the rewards will far outweigh any costs involved," Bill replied.

"I think we need to draw this meeting to a close, as there is a great deal to do. Gillian and Sir Dennis need to get themselves up to Scotland, as soon as possible. Joshua needs to do some background research to ensure that we don't get challenged from unexpected quarters. I have a scheduled meeting with the Prime Minister, in an hour's time, so I suggest we reconvene once the meeting at AB Salvage has been completed."

Bill and Gillian were the first to leave the Minister's office. Joshua and Sir Dennis were about to follow them but the Minister held them back.

"Dennis you need to keep your wits about you and I want to know everything that goes on. This project can give us so much badly needed cash, if it is successful. But if it goes wrong it would cause the Government a great deal of harm. We can't allow it to go wrong."

"Yes, Minister, I understand. I don't want to lose my job because of any failure." Sir Dennis said.

* * *

Gillian drove Bill to his rented London flat, as he hated driving through the busy city. She had recently purchased a BMW Five Series GT and was glad of the opportunity to drive it. Gillian loved cars, especially racing cars, and often went to Castle Combe, which in her opinion was the best racing circuit in Britain. One of her ambitions was to travel to France for the Le Mans twenty four hour race.

"Do you want to come up for a coffee," Bill asked as Gillian brought her car to a halt.

"Can I trust you? I expect you always invite young ladies up to your bachelor flat," she said.

This comment served as a painful reminder of Bill's reliance on prostitutes for his sexual gratification. He didn't want to tell Gillian that he was scared of trying to have any sort of relationship with a member of the opposite sex, in case they made fun of him, as the girls at University did.

"I couldn't do anything, if I tried, with this withered and useless arm," he replied with more than a hint of bitterness in his voice.

"Have I ever made any nasty remarks about your arm," Gillian said.

"No."

"Well don't treat me like one of your horrible University girls; I am much better than that. I'll take a rain check on tonight however, for there is a lot to do over the next few days, and I need my beauty sleep. Goodnight, see you tomorrow."

Once Bill was in his flat he poured himself a large glass of a twenty one year old Isle of Jura single malt whisky. He enjoyed a good whisky and always stocked several quality brands. In his opinion however, the best one was the Isle of Jura brand with its deep mahogany colour, and the smooth taste of soft fruits and berries, spice and cinnamon. *Could*

I stand a chance with Gillian? She seems different to the rest. He pushed these thoughts from his mind, as he realised there was more at stake than getting involved with a female, no matter how beautiful and clever she was.

`As Bill was finishing his second glass of whisky, he remembered what the Minister of Defence had said earlier referring to the Sussex Gold. *For the best interest of the British taxpayers, I want it back.* The warmth of the whisky was making him very relaxed, and he started to doze. *For the best interest of Bill Wyman, I want a share of the gold.* This was the last thought he had before succumbing to a deep sleep.

Chapter 8 – Lochbuie Castle

The sheet rain and driving wind swept across the open courtyard and battered the formidable grey walls of Lochbuie Castle. The three men, emerging from the Scottish baronial style castle's comfortable interior, battled with the extremely unpleasant conditions as they raced towards their parked vehicle. The chauffeur, who had been left in charge of the Rolls Royce Phantom, held the doors open for his passengers as they climbed into the car. Putting up with the adverse Scottish weather conditions was a small price to pay for the opportunity to get behind the wheel of this beautiful, luxurious car. Power was delivered from a direct injection V12 engine and, even at seventy miles an hour, ninety percent of the power was available in reserve. Pressing the accelerator always gave him a wonderful feeling as the powerful beast was then under his control. *What a machine*, he thought, as he steered towards the castle gates.

"Get us to Craignure as fast as you can," the passenger sitting directly behind him ordered. We need to catch the three o'clock ferry back to Oban."

* * *

Lochbuie Castle, situated at the head of Loch Buie on the south coast of the Isle of Mull, possessed one of the most wonderful viewpoints on the whole island. On a clear day the view was simply amazing. The first thing that caught the eye's attention was the sea otters playing in the Firth of Lorn. Golden Eagles could also be spotted hunting their prey. Continuing their journey, the eyes would come to rest on the stunning

Isle of Colonsay, with its soul-stirring, white sand stretches, lapped and lashed by intense blue seas.

The owner of Lochbuie Castle chose it as his home for neither the amazing scenery, nor the privacy that it could provide, but chose it because of the healthy population of white-tailed sea eagles on the island. Many people had come to recognise the Isle of Mull as "Eagle Island." Craig Burke loved the sea-eagle, and, with modern day communication systems and the various forms of transportation at his disposal, he didn't suffer any inconvenience from basing his operational headquarters on this Hebridean Island.

Craig Burke was an extremely wealthy man with assets worth billions of pounds sterling. His father had died, five years earlier, with stomach cancer, the world's fourth most common cancer. It has a high death rate, and even with all the medical expertise his father's wealth could buy, his death couldn't be prevented. Craig, being the only next of kin, inherited his father's large business empire.

"Do you think they will agree?" the younger of the two men crossing the front hall dominated by the red deer's stags antlers, asked. John Woodward had proven his ability and loyalty over the last three years. Craig depended on him to ensure that all their illegal activities were successfully carried out, and that nothing could be traced back to them.

"Yes, I think they will see sense once they evaluate our proposal, and consider the consequences if they reject it."

"How long should we wait for their reaction?" Craig's right hand man said.

"I think we should give them a week, for they need to contact a number of their colleagues. If there is no response by then, we will have to put Plan B into action. I've arranged some lunch for us in the dining room, so we can further discuss this on the assumption that our plans will go ahead." Craig always enjoyed taking his meals in the dining room because of the spectacular views of the garden. There would be disappointment today; however, as the extremely inclement weather currently being experienced hid the garden from view.

Craig Burke bore two special distinguishing features. He possessed one blue eye and one brown eye. With some people the depths of their spirit could be read in the wellsprings of their eyes, but this was not possible with Craig since his were cold and unwelcoming. In principle he was not a fan of body art or piercings, but he was proud of his sea eagle tattoo which decorated his right arm.

When Craig was much younger, he obtained his LLM Degree in International Law from Edinburgh University, the world's twenty-third ranked university. His father had also encouraged him to study in America, and especially wanted him to attend the Harvard Law School. Craig was always indebted to his father for this fantastic opportunity to study at this world renowned prominent law school. He graduated with a J.D. Degree in International Law. His father had been so proud of his attainment of the Juris Doctor Degree, that he put him in charge of one of his smaller companies. This gave him the opportunity to gain valuable practical experience in running a business, and helped him to attain quick progress up the management structure of his father's business empire.

It was necessary for Craig to undertake a huge amount of travel as he grasped with the enormity of his new responsibilities. He met many people from all walks of life, some of whom were involved in illicit dealings. Craig had different ambitions to his father. He was far greedier and had a greater appetite for wealth and power. Gradually he got involved with gangs who supplied weapons to mercenaries and rebel fighters. He also saw opportunities, to supply Black Market goods, when embargoes were levied against some countries. He did have some scruples however, for he would have nothing to do with either drugs or people trafficking.

"What do you know about the small arms trade?" Craig asked John Woodward as they were enjoying the warm duck salad with walnut and orange dressing. The food at the castle was always first-rate for Craig only employed the best cooks available.

"Even though this is the age of nuclear power and other weapons of mass destruction, the vast majority of all warfare continues to be conducted using conventional weapons, machine rifles, grenades, landmines, explosives and light rockets. There are many guerrilla revolutionaries and many groups defending themselves against their own violently abusive governments. We have a grand opportunity to make a great deal of money from supplying the Black-Markets of Africa, Iraq, and Afghanistan just to name a few." John replied before picking up his glass of wine.

"This Fiddlehead Cellars 2002 "Lollapalooza" Pinot Noir is an excellent match for this duck," Craig said. "I love the complex mix of dark cherry, chocolate, tobacco and subtle barnyard flavours from the Santa Rita Hills region."

"I agree."

"Getting back to the subject, I think we should concentrate on providing a supply of small arms to Africa where there is a huge demand, and only a handful of African countries have the capacity to manufacture arms and ammunition. This is why we need Chris Tenant and his colleagues to be with us. Their African distribution company has warehouse facilities scattered throughout the continent." Craig said.

"Did you hear about the Kurdish security contractor who purchased a Glock 19, one of the nine-millimetre pistols that the United States issued by the tens of thousands to the Iraqi Army and police, from an open-air grocery stand?" John asked.

"That's not an isolated incident for it is well known that in the Sulaimanya District, in Iraq illicit weapons are sold in tea houses, the back rooms of grocery kiosks, cosmetics stores and rug shops, or from the boots of cars." Before Craig could continue, his mobile telephone rang. He saw by the display that it was Bill Wyman. Craig only gave his private number to selected and trusted people. Bill was one of these as they mutually benefitted from some profitable deals in the past. Craig was relaxed about speaking to Bill on his mobile phone because he had never come under scrutiny from either the police or any other law enforcement agency. He ensured that his taxes were always paid on time, and operated an extremely tight security system throughout his operations. He was untraceable.

"Why are you phoning me on my private number, this is most unusual? Do we have a problem?"

"No problems, only an opportunity to add to our wealth." Bill knew that he was not in the same league as Craig Burke, as far as the amount of wealth that they each possessed. He was just happy for every chance to increase his.

Bill reminded him about his work with the Archaeological Review Group. He then went on to tell him about *HMS Sussex* and how it sank with a vast fortune in gold coins. "That gold could be ours," Bill continued. "It won't be an easy job in reclaiming it but I believe it can be done."

"What do you want from me?" Craig asked.

"You own a company in Greenock called AB Salvage. I want to send my assistant to meet your Managing Director to enlist his help. Gillian is an expert in Treasure Hunting and AB Salvage has the resources. It's a good combination."

"Ok, that's fine by me. Anything else you need to tell me at this stage," Craig said.

"Well there's just one problem. Gillian has to be accompanied by Sir Dennis White KCB, the Permanent Under-Secretary of State. He is to have overall responsibility for security and to ensure that there are no leaks from any member of our team."

"I'm not happy about that. He mustn't find out about me or you will live to regret it."

"I will be careful," Bill replied.

"You'd better be. Make sure that you keep me informed and take care to see that James Martindale, the Managing Director of AB Salvage, believes that this project is authorised by the Government and that there is no other ulterior motive. AB Salvage only operates within its legal boundaries and I don't use it for any of my not so legal activities," Craig continued.

"No problem. Could you contact James Martindale? Inform him about the project and warn him to expect two visitors tomorrow. If you can do that it would be a tremendous help."

After putting the phone down, Bill breathed a huge sigh of relief. *It's started*, he thought to himself.

Chapter 9 – AB Salvage

The journey to Greenock was uneventful except for the usual traffic congestion at the Kingston Bridge, which crossed the River Clyde in Glasgow. This bridge is one of the busiest road bridges in Europe, carrying around a hundred-and-fifty thousand vehicles every day. When the bridge was opened by Queen Elizabeth the Queen Mother in nineteen-seventy, the bridge was designed to handle only twenty thousand vehicles a day. The long-term attempt to take some of the local short-distance traffic away from the Kingston has not yet come to fruition, and so the car carrying Dennis White and Gillian Young joined the long queue of traffic.

It was most unusual for Dennis to be doing the driving, as a Permanent Under-Secretary of State he was normally chauffeur driven. As there was a need for the utmost secrecy however, and as The Minister of Defence had specifically put him in charge of project security, he had decided to keep the number of people involved to the absolute minimum. Although Gillian was not the type that grabbed everyone's attention when she entered a room, she was very pretty, having the sexiest brown eyes he had ever seen. He didn't find the decision hard to make under the circumstances.

"Did you know that there is a dubious urban myth that the bodies of gangsters are buried in the pillars of the bridge?" Dennis asked Gillian as they waited impatiently for the traffic to start moving. Dennis spoke with a clipped upper class accent similar to that used by BBC Broadcasters from the nineteen sixties. His voice grated on Gillian's nerves, but she did her best to hide how much she hated it.

"No, I haven't heard anything like that. Is there any truth in it?"

"My understanding is that a Glasgow godfather is supposed to have ordered the murders of several criminals, and had their bodies disposed of in the concrete piers of the bridge. An Archie McGeachy, who was twenty two when he vanished from his Govanhill Home, over thirty years ago, is rumoured to be one of the bodies. The Strathclyde Police believes he was one of a gang of four who carried out a bank raid in Williamwood, Renfrewshire."

"Have the bodies never been found?" Gillian was getting more and more intrigued and wanted further information about this fascinating story.

"No, but a bridge renovation project is soon to commence, which will involve dismantling the piers. If there are any bodies they may be discovered then."

"Traffic's moving, let's go." Gillian said.

Once over the bridge it would only take three quarters of an hour to reach their destination. Gillian wasn't looking forward to working with the Permanent Under-Secretary of State at the Ministry of Defence. She had discovered that he had a wealthy background, had been educated at Eton College and had gone on to study at King's College University, Cambridge. Dennis was so proud of his time at Eton College he seemed to ensure that it was mentioned no matter what the topic of conversation was. He told her that it was the most famous public school in the world, founded by King Henry VI. Dennis seemed to take pleasure in disclosing to her that his parents had to pay well over thirty thousand pounds per year for him to have the privilege of attending this exclusive college.
She finally stopped his boasting when she asked, "Wasn't Eton one of the independent schools investigated by the Office of Fair Trading for breaching the Competition Act?" He muttered something about a misunderstanding, but the subject was not brought up again.

* * *

"It's good to meet you. Welcome to AB Salvage." The Managing Director greeted his two visitors as he urged them to take a seat in his spacious office. James Martindale was rather obese, with a ruddy complexion. Despite having rather podgy hands he gave a very strong handshake. "During our telephone conversation, when you requested this meeting, you indicated that you were involved with a project that needs help from this company. How can we be of service?" Before either of his guests could reply James cleared his throat with his dry irritating cough. "Excuse me," he said, pouring himself a glass of water. James suffered from a disease called *Lichen Planus*, which could affect any part of the body or mouth. In his case it was confined to his mouth, making it very dry. Although much embarrassed with the symptoms of this disease he was relieved that his was only a mild case and wasn't cancerous.

"We have been given the task of conducting a major project, on behalf of the British Government, under the auspices of the Ministry of Defence. I have been put in charge of operations and Sir Dennis is accountable for project security. I understand that your company has been responsible for locating and salvaging over three hundred shipwrecks. We need that expertise as well as gaining access to the resources at your disposal."

"The aim is to find the wreck of the *HMS Sussex*, which was sunk in sixteen-hundred-and-ninety-four with its cargo of gold coins, and retrieve it before any one of a number of countries who may also be searching for it. This could be the richest shipwreck in history, and the British Government is desperate to claim the pot of gold for this country," Sir Dennis interjected.

"There are some individuals and archaeological organisations who don't want the wreck to be disturbed. There are new regulations, which govern archaeological practices in international waters, to try and protect the underwater cultural heritage. Therefore, you can see why there is a need for the utmost security," explained Gillian.

"In which part of the world did the ship go down?" James asked.

"The precise whereabouts of the ship has remained a mystery. The storm, which swept off the North African coast, caused the sea to rush into her open gun ports sinking her somewhere about one day out of Gibraltar," Gillian replied.

"There would be no quick fix to such a project and neither would it be cheap. If we were interested in committing our resources what would be in it for us?"

"As a representative of the British Government I am authorised to enter into a formal agreement with you to share the proceeds. This is the first time that any British Government is prepared to enter into such an agreement with the private sector for the archaeological excavation of a sovereign warship. Because the prize is so valuable they are prepared to enter this ground-breaking agreement," said Sir Dennis.

I do hate that voice. I'm going to have to be careful that I don't let it frustrate me enough to cause any problems with our working relationship. I need to put up with it for the sake of the project. Gillian pushed these negative thoughts from her mind before continuing the discussion. "I don't have enough knowledge to specify all the requirements we'll need, but at the very least we'll want a survey ship, cutting equipment, a diver, and some sort of submersible."

Although James knew they would need far more equipment than Gillian thought, he jotted down this list of resources before asking, "How deep do you think the Mediterranean is where the *Sussex* lies?"

Gillian looked rather thoughtful as she answered, "I'm not really sure but it's estimated that she lies at a depth of one thousand meters."

"Do you realise that the search area could cover four hundred square miles, and even if the search vessel operated twenty four hours a day, day after day, the search could take three years," James said.

Gillian and Sir Dennis were stunned into silence. They turned simultaneously to face each other in disbelief at what they had just heard. They could not afford to wait such a long time.

James noticed their concern and thought it best to quickly put them out of their misery, "Don't worry, my company has already surveyed most of the area for other projects we've worked on. I estimate that, if we accepted your invitation and can agree satisfactory terms, we could complete the necessary survey in about six months."

"Thank God for that," Sir Dennis said. "You really had me worried there for a moment. There is a lot of strong political pressure being exerted to treat this project as a matter of urgency."

"Can you come to London to meet my boss, Bill Wyman and the Minister of Defence, so that we can thrash out an agreement?" Gillian asked anxiously, relieved that James was only joking about the length of time the mapping of the sea bed could take. She now wanted to push things along to enable the project to get underway.

"I have some rather important business to conclude, over the next few days, but I can be in London next Wednesday. We can sort out the principles of an agreement then our lawyers can produce the legal framework. With goodwill on both sides I would envisage an agreement can be produced and ready for signing within a month," James replied.

"Good, we'll arrange a meeting at the Ministry of Defence when we get back." Sir Dennis said.

"Thank you, for seeing us at such short notice. It's getting late and we need to make our way back. As Dennis says we will get a meeting arranged and we'll see you next week." Gillian said

"I can arrange to put you up for the night if you would rather stay and travel back in daylight tomorrow."

"That's very tempting but we really need to get back. We'll phone you within a couple of days to confirm the time of the meeting," Gillian said, although she wasn't looking forward to sharing a car journey with Sir Dennis and his irritating voice.

Chapter 10 – Project Sussex

The Brown Pelicans, plunge diving from high overhead into the beautiful water of Magens Bay, didn't seem to know that they belonged to an endangered species. The pesticide free waters of this wonderful Caribbean Island had played a major part in their preservation, which was not the case in other parts of the world. Jim Wilson was fascinated as he watched another small flock drive fish into the shallows near the beach, and then scoop them up with their open pouches. He noticed that they were very ungainly when landing or taking off, requiring a run across the surface to become airborne. Their flight seemed to take a lot of effort, consisting of heavy flaps to gain height by soaring on outstretched wings in thermals. As Jim stood in the shallows, feeling the soft sand between his toes, enjoying the soothing effect of the gentle rippling of the water, he was amazed to see one of these strange creatures paddling towards him. It came so close to him he could see its yellow eyes and dark blue facial skin. The grey bill had a scarlet cast. *This is the life! What a beautiful island. I can see why this beach is in the world's top ten.*

Jim Wilson, a slim man with a salt and pepper beard, looked more of a geeky businessman than a swashbuckling explorer. The previous six months had been very stressful, but at last he had found some time to holiday on the beautiful Caribbean island of St. Thomas in the United States Virgin Islands. He was head of explorations for AB Salvage Limited, specialising in the field of manned and remotely operated deep-water submersibles. What he didn't know about atmospheric diving systems you could write on the back of a postage stamp. Being a hands-on leader, he often found himself in dangerous situations when dealing with undersea rescues or attempts to salvage many of the wrecks that lay beneath the oceans of the world.

Earlier that morning before coming to Magens Bay, the most popular and beautiful beach on the island, he had been catching up on some reading. Jim had an insatiable hunger for acquiring knowledge about anything to do with underwater vehicles. He was currently interested in The Turtle, the first American submarine. In 1776, with the American Revolution in full swing, the world's first submarine attack occurred. The Turtle was the invention of David Bushnell, a Yale graduate, who also invented the time bomb. The egg-shaped Turtle was a one-person submarine, barely seven feet in diameter and was operated under human power. Although it gave him a great deal of pleasure reading about such early-day submersibles, he was glad that a great deal of development had transpired over the years, and modern day vehicles were much safer, more reliable and very sophisticated.

He thought he had better check the time for he had met a young woman the day before and had arranged to meet her for lunch. "Damn, I didn't realise it was so near lunchtime," he muttered under his breath.

Every time he used his watch, he thought about his Grandfather. Robert Wilson's greatest ambition was to explore the depths of the ocean, but he suffered from Bronchiectasis, a disease that injures the walls of the airways in the lungs, which prevented him from realising it. Being so proud of the achievements of his Grandson and to help show his support he gave him this watch when Jim became Head of Explorations at AB Salvage. The Oyster Perpetual Rolex Deepsea watch with its new, patented Ringlock system could withstand depths of up to 3900 metres. Jim valued this gift greatly.

Rushing back to his room at the Bolongo Bay Beach Resort, he showered quickly. Before he could get dressed his mobile telephone rang. Joplin's ragtime music, from the sound track to the film The Sting, identified the caller as James Martindale. *I wonder what my Managing Director wants with me.* Reluctantly he answered the call.

"This better be important," ignoring the normal niceties he snapped into the mobile. "I'm having a well deserved holiday and don't want to hear about work. Besides that I'm meeting a rather attractive woman for lunch."

James had known what to expect by disturbing his friend so he didn't retaliate. He simply said, "Would you like to lead a survey to find what could possibly be the richest shipwreck in history."

"You fool, you know I would," was the immediate response. "Tell me all about it."

"I thought you had a lunch date with a beautiful woman."

"She'll have to wait. This is more important."

* * *

"What a fantastic Submarine, Admiral!" Davy Alexander, Minister of Defence, exclaimed to Admiral Sir Mark Reynolds as they discussed the virtues of the latest submarine to join the Royal Navy.

"I agree. As you know, it's our most powerful attack submarine, and I am looking forward to attending the commissioning service at the Faslane Naval Base." Mark always enjoyed these meetings at the Old War Office. Although his responsibilities swallowed a large part of his time, he still maintained an interest in architecture. He really admired this magnificent building designed in the baroque style, which had served as the centre for military affairs for so long. Some decisions that were made in this building completely changed the world forever.

"The fact that *HMS Astute* has the ability to operate covertly, and remain undetected in almost all circumstances, will be a great benefit to us," said the Minister.

"Her mix of Spearfish heavyweight torpedoes and Tomahawk land-attack cruise missiles also give us an advantage. Her sonar system is outstanding and has a range of some three thousand nautical miles. Even after all my years in the Service, I am so excited about this new submarine," Sir Mark replied with a feeling of pride, for he had significantly influenced the development of this next generation Class of submarine.

After the First Sea Lord had left, Davy started to prepare for his second meeting of the day. Although it wasn't scheduled until three o'clock, he had some preparation to do.

The negotiations that were shortly to commence were so secret that he had limited attendance to the principal parties involved. His personal assistant, Sarah, would record the minutes, but in the meantime, she was busy making sure that each place at the negotiating table had everything that was needed. He knew that his Minister for International Security Strategy and the Permanent Under-Secretary of State were already waiting in his ante-room. The last three members of this select group had not yet arrived. "I'm sorry Minister, but I have just received a telephone call. Bill and Gillian have been held up in traffic and will be twenty minutes late," Sarah informed him.

"Sarah, have you heard from James Martindale, the Managing Director of AB Salvage?"

"Yes, Minister, he travelled independently and has just checked at reception. I'll go and collect him."

"Thank you."

This was a new experience for the Minister of Defence. Most of the time he was dealing with current issues or making plans for the future. He had never considered that he would now be preparing to discuss a seventeenth century British Warship that had sunk with its cargo of gold thought to be worth billions.

He heard a gentle knock at his office door, "Come in," he said.

"Bill Wyman and Gillian Young have now arrived, Minister" Sarah informed him.

"At last," he replied rather impatiently. The Minister of Defence was not used to be kept waiting for anyone. "Usher everybody into the meeting room and I'll be there shortly."

After the usual introductions and friendly chatter, Davy very quickly got the meeting underway. He knew that any formal legal agreement would take some time to achieve. Although he wanted the project to commence without delay it was important that the negotiations delivered a watertight contract without any loopholes.

"The aim of this first meeting is to set our strategic objectives," the Minister stated. "I would also suggest that we agree a project name, and I suggest Project Sussex. Are we all agreed?" The project name was unanimously accepted.

"Can I make a suggestion for consideration," James Martindale interjected.

"Of course you can. We need to get as many ideas and discussion points listed to enable us to develop a properly-thought-out strategy. We will disagree on some of the issues raised and may not always accept them, but the more ideas we get the better." Davy replied.

"As you have requested advice and help from my company, I suggest that I arrange for the technical project plan to be produced and submitted to this group for approval," James said.

"I should have thought that would go without saying," came the frosty response from Joshua Campbell, the Minister for International Strategy.

"Now, now, we are all on the same side here. We all need to work together right from the start of this project if we are to have any success and reap the significant benefits," the Minister of Defence said rather sternly.

"Good, that's agreed. Before I put pen to paper however, can I tell you about Jim Wilson who is the Head of Explorations for my company?"

Chapter 11 – Terms stated

"He sounds as if he's the right man for the job," Davy remarked when James had finished extolling the virtues and capabilities of his Head of Explorations.

"Yes, I've the utmost faith in Jim, and he has never let me down during the many years we've worked together." Everyone in attendance was left in no doubt of the confidence James had in *his man*, and of his proven track record. They were convinced that his reliability, resourcefulness, leadership and problem-solving qualities, would make a great contribution to the success of the project.

"Thank you for updating us so eloquently. I'm sure that I speak for us all in saying that we would appreciate him being part of the team. Now has anyone else got any positive ideas or issues that they feel should be discussed at this point?" Davy asked.

"Yes, I'd like to raise some points for consideration if I may?" Bill Wyman said. He wanted to ensure that he remained central to the necessary planning required for Project Sussex. He needed to convince the gathered ensemble of his usefulness, and by doing so he would be in a much better position to meet his hidden agenda. "There are a number of archaeologists who would be worried about a project like this, and would not want it to proceed."

"I don't understand. Why would anybody not want a massively lucrative project like this to go ahead?" Josh Campbell interrupted.

"I know, from my work on the Archaeological Review Group, that there would be concerns about conservation issues. Many archaeologists would also be anxious about the preservation of the dignity of the wreck as a grave. I have experience of dealing with one particular group who moved heaven and earth to ensure that the archaeological integrity of any site was preserved. They would want our project to be an archaeological operation, rather than some sort of smash and grab with a robotic bucket on the sea floor. They would also want to know what the plan would be if human remains were found and how exactly everything will be catalogued," Bill explained.

"You're right about this. We need to be careful. I authorise you to bring all the major interested parties together by inviting them to join an advisory group under your chairmanship. You must make it clear to them that the group has no authority to make decisions, but that you will ensure their advice is passed to the appropriate authority. You will have direct access to me at all times so that you can keep me informed of their deliberations."

"Yes, Minister. I'll make the necessary arrangements," Bill said. He hid his feeling of satisfaction very well. His plan was working out just right.

"I'm confident that my company can provide all the necessary specialised equipment needed for this project and with Jim Wilson leading the on-site operation he will use them to maximum effectiveness. However, we need to agree what our payment terms will be as the initial outlay will be considerable," the Managing Director of AB Salvage said. He knew that a detailed legal agreement would need to be entered into, but he wanted to get an agreement in principle as soon as possible.

"I'm afraid we haven't got enough time available to thrash out the details of this, at this meeting. We can agree some principles and our lawyers can put the beef on the bones over the next few days. What did you have in mind?" Sir Dennis White said. As Permanent Under-Secretary at the Ministry of Defence, he was responsible for leading the negotiations in such matters.

"I would like to propose that the British Government fund the initial costs." Before he could continue, Josh Campbell brusquely interrupted him.

"That's ridiculous! You can't expect the Government to take all the risks."

"Don't forget my company is providing the technology in which we have invested a great deal. We are providing the expertise and experience gained over many years. Before you so rudely interrupt, you should hear me out. As you know the Government will accrue a huge financial return from this dive on the *Sussex*."

"Please forgive my impatience," Josh replied. He didn't appreciate being rebuked in front of his Minister although he realised he was out of order.

"Assuming that you will agree to fund the initial costs, I feel that it would be fair if my company receives the following fee. If agreed the Government would get an increasing share of the proceeds. So, on the first £25 million AB Salvage would be paid at the rate of eighty per cent, and then half of what is found between £25 million and £278 million, and forty per cent of anything above £278 million."

There was silence round the table as the details were absorbed. "You've obviously given this a lot of thought, but I can't give you an answer today. I'll contact you as soon as I can, but I don't see any problem with the principle," Davy answered.

This was a ridiculously hefty fee being demanded for providing the services and technical know-how from AB Salvage, but James was in a very strong position. He knew that no other company had anywhere near the capabilities that his company could provide. If the British Government was serious about undertaking this project they would find it difficult to reject his payment demand.

* * *

Loch na Keal has a bold and dynamic coastline of cliffs rising in landslipped tiers, unmasked by tree growth but studded with huge boulders. The route to the peak of Beinn Mhor, the highest mountain and only Munro on the Isle of Mull, starts from the island's principal sea loch on its Atlantic shore. The route follows farm tracks, the side of a stream and ultimately up scree slopes to the top. Although there is another more demanding route, climbers are still rewarded with a glorious view when they complete the four hour walk, and reach the summit.

On a clear day, the view encompasses the Sound of Mull, Staffa, Ulva, the Ross of Mull and Iona in the distance. Today, there would be disappointment for anyone who had risen early in order to make the climb to the top of this "great mountain". The September dawn had brought a cloak of mist which shrouded and obscured everything from view. This together with the cold drizzling rain would make it a very unpleasant experience for those who made it to the peak.

In the distance Craig Burke could just make out the misty outline of Beinn Mhor. This was of no interest to either him or his companion. Their eyes were transfixed on a wonderful rich red-brown creature grazing on a hillock just two hundred yards in front of them. The majestic Red Deer stag had nine point antlers, and Craig estimated that he weighed about 180 kilograms. The four hinds, which made up his harem, were slaking their thirst from a nearby stream.

Craig wasn't sure if the shudder he felt shaking his body was caused by the cold and damp ground, or the heady overwhelming excitement he felt. "It was worth starting our stalk so early when we've a chance of bagging such a fine specimen," Craig whispered as he slowly raised his Remington Model 7600 centrefire pump gun to his shoulder.

His companion was lying absolutely still, beside him, in order not to frighten their prey. "I've never been so close to a wild stag before," John Woodward breathed in reply. Neither of the two men wanted to make any noise or sudden movement that would frighten their target.

Craig lined up his shot but being uncomfortable with his shooting position, he hesitated. In that split second the wind changed and the hinds were onto them and bolted. The stag bounded away.

"Damn it," Craig cursed.

"We were so close to making the kill," John muttered disappointingly.

"I don't suppose there is any chance of catching up with the deer," John asked. He was inexperienced in the art of deer stalking, and this was the first time he had ever had the opportunity to join Craig in a hunt.

"No, I'm afraid not. They will be long gone." Seeing the skies beginning to darken Craig continued, "The wind is increasing and the rain is becoming heavier so let's go back to the bothy until the weather eases."

Although the bothy was basic in design, it provided a windproof and watertight shelter. "I'm glad we left some provisions here before we commenced the deer stalk," John said as he closed the door behind him.

"My chef filled the basket with two small flasks of Scotch Broth soup and some locally baked Wheaten Rolls stuffed with Smoked Chicken with Garlic Mayonnaise. I see that he has also put in some fruit and my favourite Scottish Strathdon Blue Cheese. Would you like a glass of whisky before we eat?" Craig said.

"Yes please. Is the whisky from the local distillery at Tobermory?"

"No, my favourite is a seventeen year old single malt from the Bowmore Distillery on the Isle of Islay. It is a special drink and I really enjoy it's mild, lingering smooth flavour."

"As our deer stalking has been unfruitful, perhaps you can update me on progress with Chris Tenant. Has he placed any orders for small arms yet?" Craig asked as he poured himself a large glass of his *Cadillac of Islay Malt*.

Chapter 12 – Preparations begin

The hot Scotch broth soon revived them from the effects of lying on the cold damp ground during their deer stalk. The special whisky also played its part in boosting their deflated spirits. "These Smoked Chicken rolls are really good. I didn't realise how hungry I was, and I'm so pleased you organised this picnic basket of goodies," John said between devouring each, very welcome, mouthful. His love of food greatly contributed to his rather podgy frame. Although three stone overweight, he was quite comfortable with it and didn't see it as a problem.

"Stop prattling on and answer my question," Craig snapped impatiently.

John knew better than to argue with his boss when he was in such a grumpy mood. *I suspect he's still annoyed about losing the stag.* "He's ordered fifty Ruger SP101 small stainless steel revolvers. He wanted a supply of small, powerful, dependable and durable handguns that were suitable for concealed carry. I recommended the Ruger SP101, as I think it is perfect for his requirement. He also wants about a hundred machine pistols."

"Has he asked for any particular make?"

"No, he has left it to me as long as the cost falls within his price range."

"What are you going to recommend?"

"I feel that the Scorpion SA 361 submachine gun will fit the bill. This Czechoslovakian machine pistol is one of the best known machine pistols in the world. It has a magazine capacity of ten or twenty rounds and can fire eight hundred and fifty rounds per minute. I know that various terrorist groups prefer it for its small size and ease of silencing. Also, it can be easily fired single-handedly, like most pistols. Yes, I think that it is exactly what Chris wants," John said.

"When does he want delivery of the weapons?" Craig asked.

"He wants them by the end of next month delivered to one of his secret warehouses in Somalia. I don't know the exact location yet, but I will receive it seven days before the actual delivery is to be made." John replied.

"Will you be able to meet his deadline?"

"Yes, I'm planning for them to be brought in from neighbouring Ethiopia. We just need the delivery date and it's all systems go."

"Good, it sounds as if you've got everything under control. We've got to make sure that nothing goes wrong with this delivery. I want Chris to gain confidence in our ability to supply whatever weapon he needs. Experience tells me that, if we do gain his confidence, he will gradually ask for larger more powerful weapons, and therefore more profit for us," Craig said.

Throughout the world, numerous state security forces were pitted against guerrillas seeking greater political autonomy. This was the market place in which Craig Burke and John Woodward operated. Government forces usually found a ready supply of weapons through the legal international arms market; insurgents generally must rely on the black-market to sustain their combat. Craig didn't care that the black-market trade in small arms and light weapons sustained bloody conflicts and armed criminals, terrorists and drug-traffickers. He was only interested in his own financial gain.

"I hope that Project Sussex is going equally well," Craig said, turning his attention to the huge opportunity for adding an enormous sum to his not inconsiderable wealth.

* * *

Dr Tom Dickson loved the sea and everything connected to it. His new life in the sun-soaked Spanish Province of Andalucía suited him down to the ground. The region boasted in excess of eight hundred kilometres of coastline and was blessed with over three hundred days of sunshine every year. After selling his Consultancy Company for what was to him a small fortune, he used it to escape from the stress of running a business. The last few years had been especially difficult as the British economy was adversely affected by a very bad recession. The inclement English weather also gave him a good reason to relocate to warmer climes.

His villa was located two miles east of Estapona, a traditional small Andalucian fishing port, situated between Marbella and Gibraltar, just at the foot of the Sierraermeja Mountains. Sheltered from the cold northern winds, it benefitted from a mild climate all the year round. He was especially pleased that the nearest beach was only five hundred yards from his front door, and led onto a small wonderful natural harbour. This was where Tom moored his Broadblue 435s2 multi hulled Catamaran. The marketing literature describe it as being a powerful, comfortable, stable and safe blue water cruiser with strikingly beautiful lines. Tom had proved this to be an accurate description and his purchase was good value for money.

Estapona had managed to preserve its peaceful town balconies with flower pots and whitewashed houses where older folks sat and chatted outside their front doors in the evening watching the passers-by as they had done for years. Tom got a lot of pleasure from just walking around, looking at the yachts and boats which were berthed in the fantastic marina. Tom now had a stress-free life. Tom was happy.

* * *

Tom made his way to La Regatta, which in his opinion, was the best bar/restaurant in the area and definitely the best value for money! Food exactly as you like it cooked and a guarantee of the best table in the place with a marina view.

"Oiga Camerero por favor," Tom said attracting the waiter's attention.

"Si Senor que va a tomar?" Now that he was being served Tom placed his order and went to his usual table.

Tom was thoroughly enjoying his Cerveza, fresh bread, cheese and Jamon de Serrano as he people-watched and mulled over the earlier telephone conversation with James Martindale. It had been a couple of years since their paths had last crossed so he was especially glad to hear from him. James was more than just a friend. He had saved his life and he would always owe James a debt of gratitude.

They had first met fifteen years previously when on independent holidays. James had joined a cave diving group who had organised a dive into the Cenote Esqueleto, otherwise known as the Temple of Doom located outside of Tulum, Mexico. Cave diving can be extremely dangerous even with the proper equipment and adequate training. Tom didn't join the group but decided to go on his own. He wanted to Free Dive, so he thought that being part of an organised group would prevent him from the chance to experience a different world, unfettered by a tank and suit.

He remembered taking a deep breath on the surface to slow his heart rate. He remembered jack-knifing downward with slow kicks to exert less energy. He remembered searching for an underwater air pocket of trapped bubble trails, from scuba divers who've gone deeper, to allow him to catch a breath to stay down longer. He remembered spotting an air pocket not realising that it was unsafe. He gulped the carbon dioxide-filled pocket and suffered a seizure on his way to the surface.

James, who was scuba diving in the Temple of Doom at the same time, spotted Tom in difficulty and managed to get to him just in time to help the struggling diver. Although Tom was unconscious, James got him to the surface without a minute to spare and dragged him out of the water. Immediately he began cardiopulmonary resuscitation, hoping to kick start a pulse. James saved Tom's life by being at the right place at the right time, and by his quick reactions.

A few days after the accident, James went to visit Tom as he recovered in the local hospital. "How are you feeling?" James asked.

"I'm doing pretty well considering. The Doctor has told me that, if you hadn't acted so quickly, I would have died. I'll always be grateful to you, and if there is ever anything I can do for you then all you have to do is ask."

"There's no need to thank me as I only did what anybody would do, but I have to say that you're a fool if you don't stop this free diving lark," James said.

"Ok, ok, don't keep on, I've learnt my lesson. I'll give it up and stick to scuba diving."

Now all these years later Tom would be able to make some repayment for the saving of his life. *I wonder why he wants to bring a boat with a diving team to Estapona.*

"La cuenta por favor." Once Tom paid his bill he made his way back to his villa. He had a lot to prepare in readiness for James and his team before they arrived in three weeks time.

Chapter 13 – The Fire

Robert and Bill were lifelong friends. Born in Greenock, they both grew up in the Larkfield District of this well known shipbuilding town. Their homes were located within a five-minute walk from the local school, which they both attended. In due course they continued their education at the same senior school, and hating the experience they left as soon as they were legally allowed. Commencing their engineering apprenticeship with AB Salvage on the same day, their paths seemed to be inextricably linked over the next fifteen years of their working lives.

Nobody could label them as alcoholics but they both had serious "drink" problems, the effects of which got them into severe difficulties with their employer. They were certainly not model employees, and their attitude to work was appalling. This led eventually to their recent dismissal, as the Company had reached the end of its patience, and couldn't tolerate their conduct any longer.

It was a horrible night, heavy rain with a cold strong wind made it extremely unpleasant for anyone venturing out from the comfort of their homes. Being a Friday, it was their usual night for going on a drinking binge ending up in the Red Dragon, their favourite haunt. The typical Greenock inclement weather wasn't going to stop them from this weekly routine, especially after losing their jobs. Once kitted out in their "wet weather gear," they set off.

As they got more and more intoxicated, they began to slate AB Salvage for sacking them. The large volume of alcohol consumed fuelled their latent anger. "We didn't deserve to be sacked just liked that," Bill angrily blurted out. His face had turned a bright red colour and the veins on his neck were standing out with rage.

"Yeah, they treated us like dirt. That Personnel Manager didn't listen to us, one little bit. I think we should get our own back," Although his speech was becoming more and more slurred it was just clear enough for Bill to make it out.

"Don't be stupid there's nothing we can do. Let's have another beer instead." Turning to the Barman, Bill ordered two more pints of Bitter.

"I know how we can get into the yard without being spotted and then we can see what we can give them for a leaving present. Finish these beers, then we'll buy some cans to take with us."

The two friends hoped the rain would ease by the time they reached the yard, but it didn't. Once inside they looked around for shelter. Robert spotted that a door to one of the large storage sheds was open. The effect of having drunk so much alcohol caused them to stagger rather than run to the shed. "God, what a terrible night," Robert moaned as he switched on the nearest light. Although his brain was getting befuddled with the effects of too much strong drink, he still had sufficient common sense to jam the door with a piece of wood to stop them being locked in, if the howling wind outside should bang it shut.

"Let's have a cigarette and a beer before we do anything," Bill said digging deep inside his protective clothing and pulling out a half full packet of Marlboro's. Over the years he had tried to give up his smoking habit, but found it impossible although he had managed to reduce his consumption to twenty cigarettes a day.

There didn't appear to be a suitable place for them to sit, so they just slumped down on the floor with their backs against the wall of the shed for support. "Do you think the night watchman will spot us in here?" Bill said whilst sucking hard on his newly lit cigarette drawing the acrid smoke deep into his lungs.

There was no reply from Robert. Bill glanced at him and found that he had fallen asleep. "Hmmm, can't hold his liquor," he mouthed.

Although they hadn't switched on all the shed lights, there was just enough visibility for Bill to see across to the opposite side. He left Robert, where he was sleeping, and slowly stumbled across the shed floor. Any flitting thought of exploring he had had soon disappeared as he felt a sudden need to relieve himself. Throwing his cigarette to the floor he did his business. By this time he was not feeling too great and a little nauseous, so he made his way slowly back to his friend unaware that his cigarette had not been extinguished.

The cigarette, with the glowing red tip, had fallen into a pile of oily rags and started to smoulder. The shed had flammable material stored throughout the building, and scraps of packing and other substances littered the floor and overflowed from bins. Flames began to leap up from where the lighted cigarette had landed on the oily rags, spreading rapidly across the floor. It seemed only seconds from the start of the fire until the non fire retardant partitions and ceiling were ablaze. Their sanctuary from the inclement weather was about to be turned into a fiery hell.

The thick choking smoke clawed at Bill's throat making it difficult for him to breath. The heat from the flames was stifling. Trying to focus through the man made fog it felt as if barbed wire was being slowly dragged across his eyeballs, causing them to stream and be really painful. The shock of his situation sobered Bill sufficiently and he was able to shake his companion awake, "Quick, let's get out of here or we'll be burnt to a cinder!"

Robert and Bill were extremely lucky not to be totally overcome by the smoke and flames. They managed to drag themselves out of the burning building seconds before the ceiling came crashing down on top of them. Gasping to get some fresh air into their smoke filled lungs the unintentional arsonists heard the loud whining sound of Police and Fire Brigade sirens. "Someone's sounded the alarm. If we go back the way we came in, we should manage to get clear without being caught," Robert said.

"That'll teach them to get rid of us," Bill foolishly commented, with a self satisfied grin on his face, as he staggered after Robert who had already started to move away from the danger area.

The close proximity of the Greenock Fire Station, at Rue End Street, enabled the Fire Tenders to reach the scene of the blaze within ten minutes. It was too late. The fire had got such a hold on the building, that no matter how hard the fire fighters tried to douse the flames, they couldn't save it.

The building was razed to the ground, and all its contents were destroyed. After struggling and failing with the main fire, the fire fighting team did have some success in stopping the fire spreading to other parts of the shipyard.

* * *

"Do we know yet what caused the fire?" James Martindale sought an explanation from his security personnel. They had been summoned to a crisis Board Meeting, early the next morning, following the disastrous accident the previous night.

"No Sir, not yet," Donald Boag replied. Donald was the Senior Security Officer. He had occupied this position for about seven years. James had always found him to be dependable and trustworthy, although he wasn't always as proactive as he should be given the responsibilities of his position. Donald had served as a Sergeant in the Argyle and Sutherland Highlanders before joining the company and ran his department with the same military precision. "My whole team, together with a fire officer who specialises in checking for arson, has been working all through the night but we haven't yet managed to determine the cause of the fire."

"Don't you have any idea? Was it an accident? Was it started deliberately?" The Managing Director was getting really agitated and frustrated that no definitive conclusions had been reached. "Contact me any time of the day or night as soon as you have some evidence as to what happened," James demanded before dismissing Donald from the Board Room.

Donald was glad to escape from the Board Room. He was not a highly educated man and didn't feel comfortable having to deal with questions in front of the company's directors. His pock marked face: sallow skin and round shoulders hid the fact that inwardly he possessed nerves of steel. Nevertheless, he was thankful to be released from the directors questioning to get on with the job in hand.

Once Donald had left the room James asked the Operations Director for his update. "As you already know the fire didn't spread, and therefore the damage was confined to Shed 31. Unfortunately however, the 25-mile-long remote control fibre optic cable for our remotely controllable deep water submersible was destroyed. Some of the specialised cameras and sonar units, which it uses, were also in the shed when it was burnt down. They too have obviously been destroyed," he reported. Karl Thompson was not a man to either mince his words or try to make bad news sound more palatable than it really was. He always got straight to the point.

"That's bad news," James said. "Is that the extent of the damage to our submersibles?"

"I'm afraid not. The thrusters had also been removed for a general overhaul...."

Before he could finish James interrupted him. "Are you saying that they have also been damaged?"

Before replying Karl took a deep breath for he knew what the effect of his answer was going to have on his fellow directors, "I'm afraid they have been put beyond repair."

"Karl, please tell me we have the necessary spares to replace the destroyed equipment?" James questioned.

"We have sufficient cameras but the loss of the sonar equipment gives us a problem. Our total supply of fibre optic cable was ruined in the fire. We can replace the mechanical parts used in the Thrusters but some of the electronic control panels will need to be re-built."

This was shocking news. Could Project Sussex be put at risk as a result of this absolute disaster?

Chapter 14 – Ambushed

St George's Wharf, an award winning riverside development being bathed in glorious sunshine, looked absolutely stunning and outstandingly impressive. Even without the benefit of such sunshine, the architecture of the building was wonderful. Although the luxurious apartments were not inexpensive, they were much sought after, as the London SW8 address was an ideal location for anyone working in the City. With the A202 crossing the River Thames over the Jubilee Bridge and the Jubilee Underground Station nearby, getting about was relatively easy. The six hundred thousand pounds which Gillian Young had inherited enhanced her own savings, to the extent that she was able to purchase one of the apartments. *Thank you, Uncle Brian*, she would often think as she enjoyed the comforts of her home.

Brian Young was killed in a multiple car crash on the M5 near to his home town of Bristol. The driver of a forty tonne fully loaded articulated lorry wasn't as focussed as the conditions on the fog bound motorway demanded. The fog caused him to underestimate the speed of his vehicle, and his ability to judge distance was also impaired. After driving for several hours the strain of staring into the thick fog made him drowsy and sapped his concentration. Suddenly realising that his vehicle had drastically narrowed the safety gap with the car in front, he reacted by forcefully jamming on his brakes. The tyres squealed and dug into the tarmac bringing the heavy load to a shuddering halt. A chain reaction accident was caused when the car driven by Brian ploughed into the back of the lorry. The grinding sound of metal fusing into metal was horrifying. Two other cars then rammed Brian's Audi A6 Saloon causing it to be concertinaed between them and the lorry which had started the whole nightmare. It wasn't a nightmare, however it was very real. People were injured. Brian Young, a Private School Headmaster on his way home, was killed instantly.

Gillian had loved her Uncle Brian. They had been very close and she missed him a great deal, but she knew she could never have afforded her wonderful flat if it hadn't been for the money he had left her in his will. One of her three bedrooms had been turned into a comfortable and well resourced study. Her involvement in numerous treasure hunting projects necessitated a great deal of research, and a large amount of it was done in this room. The report of her meeting with James Martindale, the Managing Director of AB Salvage, was still on the desk where it had lain since she had finished typing it. After washing up the utensils used for her evening meal she decided to review the report before passing it to her boss, when her telephone rang, "Hello, who is calling?"

"Hi Gillian, its James Martindale from AB Salvage. I have some bad news that I really need to inform you about," he said, not wasting time on the usual pleasantries, but immediately beginning to update her about the fire destruction of Shed 31. He told her about the loss of specialised equipment for the remotely controlled deep water submersible that was to be used in The Project Sussex Operation.

* * *

Gillian knew that her boss would be fuming when she updated him about the situation in Greenock, so she decided to drive over to his South West London flat rather than contact him by phone. *She could kill two birds with the one stone. I'll take Bill's copy of the report of the AB Salvage meeting with me.* She relished the opportunity to use her BMW 5 series GT car, despite the fact that she would have to negotiate the London traffic. She knew her boss hated driving through the city, but she simply loved to get behind the wheel of her wonderful car and drive no matter how busy the roads.

It took Gillian just over an hour to drive to Bill's flat in Surbiton. She was impressed with the substantial period house which contained the flat. She discovered that it occupied the west wing and had its own separate entrance. "Come in, come in," Bill said on opening his door to Gillian. "This is a pleasant surprise, I wasn't expecting you tonight."

"I thought I should deliver my report of the meeting with James Martindale as soon as possible. I also have some bad news and felt you should hear it face to face."

"What news?" Bill asked anxiously.

Gillian, rather hesitatingly told him about the telephone call from James Martindale, the fire, and destruction of equipment needed for the remotely controllable deep water submersible to be used for Project Sussex. His response was far worse than she had anticipated. He went ballistic.

"What! The submersible can't be used! How soon can the equipment be replaced? How much damage to the project is this going to cost? What idiot is responsible for lack of security at the shipyard?"

"Bill, calm down, it's not as bad as you think," Gillian tried to reassure him.

"What do you mean it's not as bad as I think? It's disastrous," Bill snapped back. He wasn't concerned about the interest of the British Government in trying to retrieve the gold from the sunken *HMS Sussex*; he was only interested in making sure that he was still able to misappropriate some of the funds.

"I'm sure that everything possible is being done to sort things out. James knows the urgency of the situation and will keep me informed of progress. Don't get to wound up, we need to keep everything in perspective. I'm sure everything will be alright." As Gillian tried to calm him down her memory flashed back to the night when he had invited her to his flat for a coffee. Glancing at his withered arm she was reminded of his bad experiences at University and of how bitter he was at the way girls treated him. Although she hadn't accepted his invitation she wondered if there could possibly be something between them. Despite his disability there was a magnetism about him that attracted her.

"Could I have a whisky please?" Gillian asked.

"But, you've got to drive back home."

Gillian placed her hand gently on his arm, and in a soft and sexy voice said, "Not if you put me up for the night."

* * *

The two old battered Isuzu five tonne trucks threw up a trail of dust as they rumbled towards their destination. The long arduous journey from Addis Ababa had been uneventful. Road conditions in Somalia were extremely poor to say the least so people used donkeys, camels and cattle for transportation. Mogadishu, the Somalian Capital, had witnessed heavy fighting and woeful destruction since the commencement of the Civil War in the early 1990's. The trucks however, were not headed for Mogadishu but were bouncing and bumping their way along the rough dirt track road towards Baardhere, an important agricultural city in the Gedo region. Chris Tennant, the gun runner, had arranged for the trucks to deliver their precious cargo to his warehouse. They would be distributed, from there, to the various militias fighting against the Transitional Federal Government. Within a few days of the gun shipment arriving, Chris was expecting to give a demonstration of a Scorpion SA 361 submachine gun to one of the pirate gangs that operate along the coastline.

The hands of the driver of the second vehicle were tight around the steering wheel, as he battled to keep his vehicle from being overturned when his tyres hit the innumerable rocks and potholes in his path. His arms and shoulders also ached from the strenuous struggle. He was about to bring his vehicle to a halt to enable the second driver to relieve him, so that his aching body could have a rest. Perhaps, once in the passenger seat he could even get some well deserved sleep. Suddenly, and without any warning, there was the sound of machine gun fire. He saw the lead vehicle slew to a halt as its tyres were cut to ribbons by a hail of bullets. Four men, including the driver, jumped from the first truck and fled for their lives. Before they could reach the sanctuary of the nearest cover, the deathly rain of bullets cut them down. Their very life force oozed from their bodies as they fell to the ground in a bloody heap.

Everything happened so very quickly. The driver of the second vehicle braked hard and stopped his vehicle before it crashed into the bullet ridden vehicle in front of him. The shock of the unexpected attack mesmerised him and he froze staring out of the windscreen. Unable to move he watched the flashes from the ambusher's gun muzzles, which were now firing in his direction. Puffs of dust were flicked up by the bullets as they exploded on the rutted track. He was still transfixed by the scene from his windscreen, when the hot metal of a machine gun bullet smashed into his skull killing him instantly.

Chapter 15 – Craig Burke's problems

"Cease firing! Cease firing!" No response. The reverberating noise of incessant gunfire, from the soldier's weapons, made it difficult to hear the order. From their hidden fire positions they continued to let loose a deadly rain of hot metal bullets at the two vehicles. Even if silencers were being used the soldiers wouldn't have responded as they were caught in the grip of a "killing frenzy."

CEASE FIRING! CEASE FIRING! I ORDER YOU TO CEASE FIRING! Captain Dalmar screamed at the top of his voice. Smashing his handgun onto the skull of the nearest soldier, he got their attention and his undisciplined militia finally responded to his order. What they lacked in professionalism however, they made up for with a blind commitment to carrying out whatever they were told to do, no matter how distasteful.

The body lying next to the lead vehicle twitched. Without waiting for an order, one of the soldiers lifted his AK-47 and fired.

Moving from the protection of the rocks, where he had deployed his men, Captain Dalmar walked slowly towards the carnage which lay thirty yards further up the dirt track road. He counted six bodies in total. Looking back towards his men, he called to his Sergeant, "Aziza, bring some men, check the bodies of the gunrunners, and make sure they are all dead. After that, search each one to see if they are carrying anything useful."

A few minutes later, Dalmar was just about to issue an order to his radioman, when he saw Aziza unsheathe his large blackened blade hunting style knife with the woven handle. "What are you doing?" he snapped as he saw the blade being thrust into the mouth of one of the dead bodies. Aziza seemed oblivious to his Captain, continuing to dig his blade into the gums of his victim. His grisly task was soon finished. Wiping the bloodied blade on the shirt of the violated corpse, he then stood up and turned to face his commanding officer.

"Look Sir, gold teeth. He had two gold teeth." Wrapping the teeth in a cloth he shoved them into a small black pouch which was attached to his bandolier. The Captain found this practice distasteful but couldn't interfere. The soldiers had to supplement their meagre pay somehow. Often they acted like vultures, descending on a kill, stripping their enemies' dead bodies of anything of value.

"Taban, get me the General on the radio." General Ismail Qasim Naji, the Commander in Chief of the Transitional Federal Government, had ordered the ambush. One of the informers from his extensive spy network had reported the illegal gun shipment and supplied the route the shipment would take. Government soldiers were not properly equipped with reliable weapons. Therefore, the cargo of Scorpion SA 361 submachine guns and Ruger SP101 small stainless steel revolvers would be put to good use.

Eventually radio contact was established. "Operation Scorpion successfully accomplished, General. They didn't stand a chance and we have no casualties," Dalmar reported with a smug smile of satisfaction.

* * *

Wolfgang Amadeus Mozart was a musical genius whose music Craig Burke loved, and he could listen to it all day if it were possible. Craig didn't believe in the "Mozart Effect" theory that was being promulgated in the newspapers. *How could listening to music make you smarter, he questioned?* Over the years however, he found Mozart's music not only gave pleasure, he found that it always brought a feeling of calmness and kept his devils at bay. He whole heartedly agreed with the sentiments that Tchaikovsky once expressed, "Mozart is the highest, the culminating point that beauty has attained in the sphere of music." But not even the sound of the wonderful

Piano Concerto No. 21, filling the Lochbuie Library with its magic notes, could do anything to quell his anger and deep frustration, when he was updated on the progress of two of his major projects. Storming over to his Burmester 069 CD player he switched it off. His full attention could now be given to the interrogation of John Woodward, who had been the messenger of the devastating news.

"How could that have happened? Information about the guns was supposed to be restricted to as few trusted people as possible. Is there a traitor in our organisation or that of Chris Tenant? You also say that Project Sussex is suffering a delay due to a fire at AB Salvage. What is going on John, these problems are costing a great deal of money?"

There is an undercurrent of unease running through the music of the Mozart Piano Concerto. John felt such unease, as he now faced the full brunt of the wrath of his boss. As Craig vented his feelings John began to feel more alarmed at what could happen. When really angry and annoyed Craig had a unique way of focussing his eyes, one of which was brown and one was blue, to give an intimidating cold and menacing stare. When a person was transfixed by such a stare, there was no way to hide the truth as it seemed to have the power to detect lies.

Attempting to take the heat out of the situation, John tried to show that he had a grip of the situation and could implement corrective action, "I can't answer all your questions, boss, but I have set the wheels in motion to discover who leaked the information about the gun shipment. You can be assured that we will find whoever did it. I've spoken to Chris Tenant and both of us feel that the informer works for him, but I'll conduct a thorough investigation and not make any assumptions. Don't worry about the Sussex Project it's only suffered a temporary setback, although I'm not sure yet how long it will take to get back on track."

"DON'T WORRY! DON'T WORRY! Of course I'm worried. Our organisation has been infiltrated and put at risk. The sooner you find the informant the better so that the leak can be stopped. Also, get in touch with Bill Wyman and find out what's happening with Project Sussex."

* * *

A few days after the night Gillian Young had stayed at his Surbiton flat, Bill Wyman still couldn't believe his luck. They had made love. Over the previous five years their working relationship had been really good, but in all his wildest dreams he never imagined that they would ever be so intimate. He had come to rely on her for she was the best assistant he had ever employed. She was the best in her chosen field of expertise and she had the sexiest brown eyes he had ever seen. He would call her later, but now he had to get on with the pre-arranged meeting with the representatives of various British archaeological societies. The Council for British Archaeology and English Heritage were also represented at the meeting. Some of these bodies had expressed concerns, to the British Government, when they heard about the intention to carry out a dive on *HMS Sussex*.

Davy Alexander, the Minister of Defence, who was in overall charge of Project Sussex, knew that these archaeologists would cause trouble. The project could be hindered if they were allowed to run amok. Bill Wyman had been authorised to hold regular discussions with them. It was felt the archaeologists could be managed if they were made to feel that they played an important part in the operation.

"Well gentlemen, I would like to welcome you to our first meeting regarding the proposed Government operation to salvage *HMS Sussex*. I must make it clear, right from the beginning, that we perform an advisory function only. I must stress that we are not a decision making body. The objective of this meeting is to produce a list of relevant topics that can be debated and incorporated into a formal agenda." Before Bill could continue the door opened and Sir Dennis entered the room.

"I'm sorry for being late, my invitation didn't arrive and I have just been informed," he said in his annoying clipped upper class accent.

Bill knew that he had never sent the invitation. He wanted to keep Sir Denis from finding out too much, as he reported to the Minister of Defence. Davy Alexander was certainly the last person on earth that Bill wanted to learn about his secret plan. Bill kept his self composure, despite his annoyance and said, "Take a seat Sir Dennis and I'll introduce you. This is Sir Dennis White KCB, Permanent Under-Secretary of State at the Ministry of Defence. Sir Dennis and I are working closely on this operation."

After an exchange of pleasantries, between the assembled group and Sir Dennis, the meeting resumed, "Now, as I was saying, we need to formulate an agenda to steer our discussions. I would like to circulate this list of suggested topics for discussion. If you wish anything else added then you present your suggestion after you have studied the document." The initial suggestions of topics were as follows;

1. Guidelines for recording items found
2. How will the dignity of the wreck as a grave be preserved?
3. The funding of future conservation

Quite a detailed and, at times, heated debate then took place, but after two hours no final agreement had been reached. Bill decided to adjourn the meeting for a week, to allow further research and clarification on any of the issues raised. As he was drawing the meeting to a close he couldn't get Sir Dennis out of his mind. *How am I going to deal with him? He could spoil this for me?*

Chapter 16 – Conspiracy at "The Three Sisters"

The Blacks were a Scottish couple who had spent a large part of their working lives travelling the world. George had been a tremendously sought after high profile International Business Consultant most of his career. Many major international conglomerates, when considering mergers or acquisitions, contracted him as a result of his many proven successes. George was very thorough when planning a project; never leaving anything to chance he was always careful to ensure that all details were carefully considered before he would press the "Green" button. Being extremely focussed and self-motivated nothing could deter him once his project was underway.

Another of his specialities was in the field of large company restructures and his expertise had saved companies many millions of pounds. Continued success had brought George huge financial rewards. Two years earlier, on celebrating his sixtieth birthday, he had decided to take early retirement. This might have seemed a radical choice for such a successful businessman to make, but it was a target he had set at the outset of his career. Boredom or bad health had no part to play in this life changing decision. George loved his work challenges and the busier he had been the better he enjoyed it. Resolving complicated business problems brought him much satisfaction and the pressure never seemed to cause him any difficulties. The word stress was not part of his vocabulary. One of his particular skills was in the area of man management. George would always admit that he enjoyed getting people to do what he wanted but achieving is not always easy. Motivating people to do and achieve tasks that either they didn't want to do, or felt they didn't have the capabilities, was indeed a true skill.

Having a life outside his extremely busy work schedule helped tremendously to keep the unremitting pressures at bay. He carried his sixty two years very well. His full head of white hair was the only clue to his age for other than that he was extremely fit, and worked out each day in his own private gym. The gym had been built, in readiness for his retirement, as an addition to the indoor swimming pool project that he had already completed. This had always been part of his plans when he had purchased the large house in Richmond, with its one and a half acres of land. Retirement would bring new opportunities. He had simply wanted to do something different.

Margaret had also travelled a great deal although not to the extent that her husband had. Most of Margaret's travelling was because of holidays or to visit family and friends. One of their three children lived in Australia with another in the United States of America. One remained in England. Whilst George was the International Businessman, Margaret successfully ran her own company. Margaret was much younger than her husband and had not yet reached the retirement stage. She was a Restaurateur and managed three restaurants under the banner of her operating company RSL. The company boasted a strong management team who looked after all day to day matters thus giving Margaret the freedom to concentrate on future strategy. This also allowed her to have more free time to share with her husband. Being very ambitious she was always looking for opportunities to expand her empire. Convincing her husband that he should use some of his accumulated wealth to help her purchase and open a new small first class restaurant, in the heart of the city of London, would not be easy. At first George objected, but the quietly spoken, strong willed and decisive Margaret managed to help him see her vision. She never doubted that they could attract Michelin Star Chefs and make it into a real success.

Soon after the decision was made matters progressed rapidly and everything went as planned, but when there had been only two months to the opening a name had still not been chosen.

"Have you decided on a name for the new restaurant," George asked one night.

"Yes, I've been giving it a great deal of thought recently," Margaret replied. "One of our favourite places is the Blue Mountains, in New South Wales. We love going there; the view by the Three Sisters is wonderful. So I feel we should call our new restaurant, The Three Sisters."

"That's a great choice. Yes, we've been very fortunate any time we visit there we always have good weather. Except for the last time when we took our friends. We couldn't see two feet in front of us, never mind view the rock formation."

"I know that was so disappointing but I still feel that's what we should call the new restaurant." The name was agreed and the restaurant, with its Michelin Star graded chefs, soon earned a fantastic reputation for providing excellent quality food.

Bill Wyman had cultivated a taste for fine dining and thoroughly enjoyed dining at The Three Sisters. The layout of the dining area suited his needs perfectly. Wonderfully white table cloths, sparkling crystal glasses with highly polished silver cutlery helped to create a comfortable and relaxing environment. Unique lighting had been specially designed to create a warm atmosphere. There was no overcrowding with the tables having plenty of space between them. Several little cosy alcoves provided privacy for diners who wished to converse without being overheard. Bill had become quite a regular and was on first name terms with the owner. He was always very appreciative of the excellent service and wonderful food that he never left without personally thanking Margaret.

Margaret, of course thought that he was very charming. Her opinion would have changed if she only knew what was on his agenda for discussion with his guest. In reality, Margaret knew very little about him, except she thought that he worked for some advisory group to the Government, on Archaeological matters.

Bill had pre-booked one of the secluded alcove tables for two persons. He had arrived alone but was expecting his guest to arrive shortly. He was just considering the menu and wondering what delight he would choose when his guest arrived. The man, whom he only knew as Jack, was led to his table by a very pretty waitress with a beautiful warm smile. Her trim athletic figure was shown off perfectly with the snugly fitting tartan dress style uniform exclusive to The Three Sisters. He knew she was originally from Thailand for he had tried to proposition her one evening, but with no success. Although he suffered this rejection he found her smile so irresistible that he was always pleased whenever she served him.

The menu was grudgingly laid down whilst Bill shifted his gaze to his guest, "Sit down Jack, sit down. Make yourself comfortable." Bill made no effort to stand to welcome his guest. Neither was there any attempt to proffer his hand in welcome. Jack may have been his guest but he was certainly not a friend. This meeting was strictly for business.

There was nothing special or distinctive about the features of the man known as Jack. He looked a pleasant every day type of guy who would just blend into any background. There was nothing sinister about his outward appearance, but underneath the surface he was as cold as ice. Emotions were not part of his personality. He could destroy people, either mentally or physically, and it would mean nothing to him. Money was his God and he got paid well, very well, for he was the best. When he carried out a hit there was never any evidence left behind. He was the ultimate discrete professional.

"As you are not used to coming to a place like this, shall I choose for both of us?" Bill said in such a way that it implied that he was the superior.

"I only want to hear what you need me for, but if it helps your deception then go ahead."

Bill signalled to the young Thai waitress. "Are you ready to order Sir," she enquired.

"What do you recommend?"

I would suggest the Lobster and Shellfish Salad with the Avocado and Vine ripened Tomato Jelly, to start. Then I would suggest the Milk fed Rack of Lamb roasted in the Salt Dough Crust, with the Lamb Compote and Shallots Pie with the stuffed Courgettes and Provencal Jus," she said without hesitation for she knew that her choices were restaurant specialities.

"That sounds fine. We will both have the same, thank you."

After the starter arrived and they had begun to eat, Bill came straight to the point, "I need you to arrange for someone to have an accident."

"Do you really mean an accident or do you mean something more?" Jack queried after taking another mouthful of the wonderfully cooked lobster.

"I don't want the target to be permanently removed from the scene, but I do need the target to be hospitalised for some time. That's why I have come to you again. I know that you're both good and discrete."

"When do you want this to happen?" Jack asked.

"Sometime within the next seven days would be perfect."

"You know my usual fee is ten thousand pounds plus expenses, is that acceptable to you?"

"Yes, I accept. I will pay you five thousand in advance and the remainder on completion of the job." Bill said.

"That is not acceptable I want the full ten thousand pounds paid up front or there is no deal." Jack demanded.

Bill took a few minutes to think before replying. There was so much at stake that he couldn't take the risk of anything putting Project Sussex in jeopardy. "Ok, I agree to your conditions. Do you want the money paid in cash?"

"No, I will give you a special Swiss bank Account from where I can arrange any further transfers to be untraceable. The money must be in this account by 4pm tomorrow." Jack responded.

Bill slipped a small envelope across the table as they were speaking. "This is the targets name with all the essential information you'll need."

Jack picked up the envelope and slit open the sealed flap. Without removing the contents of the envelope he glanced quickly at the heading on the notepaper. Four words appeared in black bold type, TARGET—SIR DENNIS WHITE.

Unknown to the conspirators Margaret had been watching them for the last ten minutes. Although she couldn't hear their conversation her sixth sense told her something unusual was going on. *What's Bill up to,* she thought.

Chapter 17 – One obstacle removed

By the time the fourth London taxi failed to stop for the solitary figure, frantically trying to flag them down, he decided to walk. At least he decided to walk as far as Leicester Square. Large numbers of people were always bustling about here, so taxis were numerous and frequent. This wasn't the first time he had walked from his club to Leicester Square. Fortunately he knew a short cut that would save him twenty minutes. Fastening his overcoat for protection against the light but chilly wind, he set off. Three men in a parked black car, hidden in the shadows, watched him in silence.

Glancing at his Omega Seamaster Professional watch he saw that it was five minutes past three in the morning. Sir Dennis White didn't usually stay at his club so late, but he had been having a great time reminiscing with an old friend. His friendship with John was formed when they both joined a group of students touring France one summer. As the years passed their friendship grew stronger and deeper. They now regarded each other as "best friends." Due to work pressures and other commitments they had not seen each other for about three years, so it had been good to catch up. "That was a first class meal and the wine was pretty good too," John said as they moved to the comfort of the club lounge for some after-dinner drinks. They were both partial to a whisky or two, and the club kept an excellent selection.

"Yes, I enjoyed it too. I've never been disappointed with the quality of food and I've been a member for a good number of years," Sir Dennis replied.

The time seemed to fly by, but eventually Sir Dennis realised he was getting rather inebriated and needed to go home. John didn't want to leave. "The night's still young, stay and have a few more drinks," he said as his friend prepared to leave.

"No, I must go, it's been a great night and it was good to meet you again. I have a special meeting with the Minister of Defence tomorrow afternoon so, I need to make sure I have a clear head."

"Thanks for the meal. I'll call you next week and maybe we can arrange to do this again," John said as his friend was preparing to leave.

The sound of the car doors being closed was almost imperceptible. Although the three men were not always so careful, they didn't want to attract the attention of their target, with the noise of a banging door echoing down the mainly deserted street. Sir Dennis continued down the small side street which ran adjacent to the back of his club, unaware of the men following him. It was unusual for alcohol to have much of an effect on him. He always boasted that he could handle his drink, but the liberal quantity consumed earlier was now beginning to affect his progress. His pace slowed and he began to stagger just as he tried to cross an alleyway. The darkness of the night made it difficult to see the kerb. It was probably the effect from the number of whiskies, he had drunk, however that caused him to misjudge his step. Not being in full control of his faculties he was unable to stop himself from falling, when he tripped on the kerb. He went down like a ton of bricks. Although not knocked unconscious, when his head smashed into the hard immovable concrete, he was both shocked and dazed. He lay spread-eagled where he fell.

The three men now saw their opportunity. Breaking into a run they rushed towards their target. Oblivious to the approaching men Sir Dennis struggled to push himself into a sitting position. He couldn't make it and collapsed back onto the pavement. Before he could manage another attempt, they were upon him, like a pack of hounds ravaging an exhausted fox.

His body became a human punch bag as fists and heavy boots smashed into it. One of the men straddled his chest and rained blow after blow to his face and head, rocking it savagely from side to side. Blood from his badly beaten nose and mouth flowed profusely down onto his clothes. When his jawbone was broken by the incessant punching, he didn't feel it. The pain was masked by more excruciating agony surging up from his ribs, when each heavy booted kick landed. The sudden vicious attack prevented Sir Dennis from having any chance of identifying his assailants, or even knowing how many there were. All he knew was pain, sickening pain that gripped him like steel bands squeezing the very life out of him. He desperately wanted it to stop. One of the men broke off from the attack and moving back a few steps retrieved his baseball bat from where he had left it until needed. They had been instructed to do a fair bit of damage so that their target was incapacitated for some time, but they were to stop short of killing. When the leader saw his companion with the baseball bat he ordered "Break both legs."

When the first hammer blow shattered the Tibia of his right leg, Sir Dennis passed out. Being unconscious gave him some immediate respite from the pain, although his punishment didn't stop until his left kneecap had been smashed by the baseball wielding henchman.

Sir Dennis White KCB, Permanent Under-Secretary of State at the Ministry of Defence, tried to fully open his eyes but couldn't. They were a mess. Heavy bluish black swelling and numerous lacerations had closed his left eye completely. The right eye was not as badly injured and allowed some vision. He could just make out a shadowy figure adjusting some sort of apparatus. It didn't register where he was. He felt so confused. His head felt as if Borneo Headhunting Drummers were banging out their rhythms on his skull, and his mouth felt as dry as the hottest desert. He tried to speak but the extent of his injuries prevented him, "Aaaaagggghhhh!!"

The Doctor turned towards the hospital bed when she heard the anguished groan. "Don't worry you're in good hands now. You've been badly hurt, but you'll live," Dr, Claire Trethowan, Consultant Orthopaedic Surgeon said in her broad Australian accent. "A postman who had only just started his round found you lying badly beaten in a side street. He dialled 999 for an ambulance. The Paramedics put your legs in splints and then brought you here to University College Hospital, at Regents Park. You will have difficulty speaking at the moment as you have suffered a broken jaw. Your ribs have been badly bruised but the worst damage is to your legs. I have given you an injection to help with the pain. Your right tibia has been broken and your left kneecap will need to be replaced. I have arranged for you to be taken to theatre at ten o'clock in the morning so that I can deal with your injuries. The damage done to your body can be repaired, but I must warn you that it will be quite some time before you will be able to go about your normal business. I apologise for being so blunt but it's important that you know the full extent of your injuries. I realise that it is a lot for you to take in just now, so I will come back before you go to theatre, when I can tell you what I am going to do." As Claire finished speaking, the drugs Sir Dennis had been given earlier started to take effect and he fell asleep.

Claire Trethowan was not only an excellent technical surgeon but she had a wonderful "bedside" manner, she really cared about patients and how they were treated. She was extremely proud of her Cornish heritage, but she had been born in the beautiful Australian city of Melbourne. She was an Aussie through and through. Ever since she was a small child her passion and burning ambition was to be a Doctor. When an opportunity came to attend Monash University it was grabbed with both hands. Fully committing herself to her studies, with just the occasional timeout for the odd party, she eventually obtained her medical degrees. After qualifying, she accepted a number of hospital appointments, in various parts of Australia. This allowed much experience to be gained whilst developing her specialism. Her reputation and career rapidly progressed helping to achieve her goal of becoming a Consultant Orthopaedic Surgeon. When she was approached to accept a consultancy at the "The Avenue", a private hospital in Malvern, she was overjoyed. This modern hospital, in one of Melbourne's exclusive suburbs, was well resourced with the very latest equipment.

After leaving the hospital she went straight home to her Chelsea flat, where she lived with her Australian husband, Lindsay. They had come to England three years earlier, as Lindsay had commenced a small property company and wanted to see it established before leaving it under the control of a Managing Director. Once this was accomplished they could go back home to Australia. He had set a target of five years to complete his objective. Claire always planned to go with him although she didn't want to give up her career. Luck was on their side however, for Claire had been able to arrange an exchange with another Consultant. These exchanges were quite common in the medical community and were of mutual benefit as both parties gained valued experience of working practices in another country. This arrangement meant that she could join her husband in London, without damaging her successful career.

When she finally got home after negotiating the heavy London traffic she found a large bunch of roses had been delivered. She loved all flowers but was especially fond of roses. Lindsay had returned to Australia to deal with some business issues, but he had remembered that it was her birthday and had arranged for the flowers to be sent. She would have a quiet night in; admire her flowers, have a glass of her favourite red wine and settle down with her new thriller book "The Startled Rabbit" by R.T. Cunard (no relation to descendants of Sir Samuel Cunard of steam ship fame). This would take her mind off her new patient for a few hours. *How could anyone be so cruel and cause so much damage to a person?*

Meanwhile Bill Wyman's expected telephone call was received. It was short and to the point but it told Bill all he needed to know.

"Job accomplished," Jack said in a cold matter of fact voice.

Before Bill got a chance to ask any questions, Jack hung up.
Bill was so relieved that what he had seen as a potential problem had been dispensed with. He wouldn't now need to worry about having a spy in the camp reporting back to Davy Alexander, the Minister of Defence. Bill would have more freedom of movement within Project Sussex, so that he could manipulate matters to misappropriate a large part of the gold hoard, lying on the seabed, in the hold of *HMS Sussex.*

Chapter 18 – Progress made

Buzzing about the Minister's office Sarah checked that everything was ready for his important meeting. Being the personal assistant to the Minister of Defence it was her responsibility to ensure all the practical requirements for any meetings he had called, were organized. She ticked off the items on her mental checklist one by one. *Notepads and pens in place-yes. Minister's fridge fully stocked with water and other soft drinks-yes.* It could be thirsty work when debating and discussing important or contentious issues, especially if deliberations dragged on for any length of time. Other Ministers kept a supply of good quality red and white wine available, but Davy Alexander had banned any form of alcohol from his office. He held a strong view that nothing should be allowed to befuddle the mind when major matters were being considered. A clear head needed to be maintained at all times. The drinking of wine or any other alcoholic beverage should be only consumed when the working day had finished, he believed. *Bowl of fruit on side table-yes. Cheese and biscuits ready-yes.*

All that remained was for her to place the two small floral arrangements on the large American Black Walnut Barrel Shaped Board Room Table and everything was ready. The Minister always wanted things to be right, to be professional. Sarah understood this and carried out her duties to a very high standard. As an afterthought, she re-counted the place settings once more to make sure that no one was missed. Her instructions indicated that places for six people would be required, and six places there were. If Sarah had known about the attack on Sir Dennis White she would only have set places for five but she was completely unaware of his misfortune.

Shortly before the Project Sussex meeting was due to commence Joshua Campbell, Parliamentary Under-Secretary of State and Minister for International Security Strategy, received notification about the attack on Sir Dennis White. This was really bad news and the Minister of Defence had to be informed immediately. Picking up the telephone he called the Minister on his internal direct line, "I am sorry to bypass Sarah, Minister, but I need to see you right away, it's a matter of some urgency."

Davy Alexander knew that Joshua wouldn't have phoned him directly if it wasn't important. "Come straight up, we've got about twenty minutes before our meeting with the Project Sussex Team starts."

The Minister was devastated when informed of the bad news. "How could anyone be so evil as to make such a vicious attack? Do we know how much damage has been done? How long will he be in Hospital? Have the police any idea who committed this terrible attack on a defenceless man?" The questions came thick and fast from the enraged Minister of Defence. Davy Alexander didn't often visibly show his anger, but his colleague and friend didn't deserve to be brutally treated in such a sickening manner.

"I'm sorry, Minister, I can't answer any of your questions, it's too early as the attack only happened in the early hours of this morning. I'll update you as soon as more information is available. I think it is safe to say however, that Dennis will not be able to continue on the Project Sussex Team," replied Joshua.

"We haven't time to continue this conversation. The other Project Sussex Team members will be in the ante-room and we really need to get the meeting started. We will bring this situation to the attention of the team during our meeting. Can you ask Sarah to send them in?" the Minister said.

The Project Sussex Team members filed in, one by one, led by Bill Wyman from the Archaeological Review Group. His assistant Gillian Young followed close behind. The Managing Director of AB Salvage, James Martindale was last to take his place. The Minister of Defence and his Minister for International Security Strategy, Joshua Campbell, were already seated. The Minister rose to shake hands with his team members and then after the usual formalities, and normal chit chat, the meeting got underway.

"I expect you're wondering why Dennis isn't present at our meeting. Well, it is with regret that I have to inform you he has suffered a savage beating and is now in hospital. We are not yet sure of all the facts. We don't know how long he will be incapacitated for. We think however that he will not be able to continue with the Project as it could be several months, or even longer, before he is able to fulfil his responsibilities." The Minister's opening remarks were met with gasps of surprise and shock from those team members who had heard this unwelcome news for the first time.

If Bill Wyman had been an actor he would have deserved to win an Oscar for his performance. He managed to convey a feeling of surprise and shock, at the news of this latest development, whilst inwardly hiding a smug feeling of satisfaction. Then panic set in as the Minister continued.

"I haven't had much time to think about it yet, as I was only informed of this terrible incident shortly before our meeting commenced, but I will need to nominate a replacement for him."

This would cause disruption to Bill's plans. *No! No! This can't happen.* He thought as his brain went into overdrive. Sir Dennis White had been getting too involved with the detail of the Project. He had already accompanied Gillian when she initially went to AB Salvage. Bill had always suspected that the Minister wanted someone, under his direct control, to keep him personally updated prior to any Project Group meetings.

"Minister, this is really bad news and I'm sure that I speak for everybody here when I say that I'm really sorry for what has happened. Sir Dennis had a lot to contribute to the project and didn't deserve to be removed from it in such a horrific way. I can assure you however that Gillian, James and I can co-ordinate matters and manage the project as far as all technical and operational matters are concerned. If both you and Joshua deal with all legal agreements and any international requirements I will ensure that you are kept fully updated. I feel that we could face further unnecessary delays to Project Sussex if someone else is brought in at this stage. There is also of course, as you yourself often remind us, for the need to maintain tight security. I strongly feel that the fewer number of people who know about this the better." Bill was at his most persuasive and had put on another great acting performance.

Whilst Bill had been presenting his case the group members had remained silent. This silence continued for a few minutes after he had finished talking. Then the Minister, who had been giving careful consideration to what had been said, gave his reply. "You're right, it is too late to bring in someone else, I agree with what you said and we'll move forward on that basis. Now, let's move to the next agenda point."

Bill could hardly contain himself. It would all have been for nothing, if Sir Dennis had been replaced. He had won. What a relief.

"I can now inform you," Joshua Campbell reported. "That the proposed financial terms between AB Salvage and the Government, which was highlighted at an earlier meeting, has now been incorporated into a formal legal contract. This contract has gone back and forth, between the Governments solicitors and those of AB Salvage being reviewed and amended, for some time. Four days ago, final agreement was reached and the contract has now been signed by both parties."

"Thank you, Joshua," the Minister said. "Now James can you tell us if the material which was destroyed in the fire at your shipyard has yet been replaced."

"I'm pleased to report that my Operations Director has now managed to replace the 25-mile-long remote control fibre optic cable for our remotely controllable deep water submersible. We now have stock of all equipment needed including cameras and sonar equipment. All repairs will be completed by the end of next week."

"What is the next step after the repairs have been completed," the Minister interjected.

"Well Minister, the submersible and appropriate equipment will need to be shipped out to Dr. Tom Dickson. He was expecting the submersible several weeks ago but obviously the fire, and subsequent damage, delayed this. I have already been in touch with him, and he is starting to make the necessary arrangements at his end. I have also taken the liberty of arranging for my Head of Explorations to fly out to help Tom Dickson as soon as he can get a suitable flight." James said.

In an effort to demonstrate that the team was gelling together Bill said, "Minister, James and I have had an earlier discussion and we both feel that it would be a good idea to send Gillian, my assistant, to Andalucía with Jim Wilson. This would give us a very experienced team used to dealing with similar type projects."

"Yes, that does sound a sensible thing to do. I'll leave you to make all the arrangements. Now, can you tell us if anything of importance came from your meeting with the various British Archaeological Groups and English Heritage?" The Minister was keen to learn if there was any imminent risk to the project, from any action these groups may be considering.

"We had a lengthy discussion but have not come to any agreement yet. I tried to anticipate their concerns and submitted a draft agenda for their consideration. I informed them that they could include additional subjects but I feel that they will stick with the three current agenda points. I have not yet set a date for our second meeting, but I will need to do it soon."

"It would be helpful if you could tell us what the three current agenda points are," Joshua Campbell requested.

"The first point relates to producing guidelines for recording any items found. As you know Archaeologists have a great concern regarding the preservation of the dignity of any wrecks as a grave, if any bodies are involved. This issue will be the second point on our agenda. Finally the funding of future conservation needs to be discussed," Bill continued.

"I feel that we are getting our basic structure into place at last. This is good progress, except of course for what happened to Dennis. There is one area that we have not tackled yet. We need to open discussions with the Spanish. As the wreck is in their territorial waters they'll want to get their hands on some of the gold. I know that any such discussions should be the responsibility of the Foreign Office but I want you to be in charge of this Joshua. I will inform the Foreign Secretary and instruct him to give you whatever assistance you need. I will also ask him to arrange an initial introductory meeting with the Spanish Ambassador here in London.

Joshua was pleased with this added responsibility. He already knew a number of Spaniards in the Government and various Ministries through his work as Minister for International Security Strategy. It would be good to renew acquaintances. More importantly however, it would do his career prospects no harm.

"I think we have covered all we need for the present. From your positive contributions to our meeting I am feeling optimistic about the success of Project Sussex. The potential financial benefit, to this country, is enormous and although this places a great burden of responsibility on our shoulders I have the utmost confidence in this team. Gentlemen, just before I close the meeting I would like to give you my personal "Thanks" for your continued dedication to this project, and for everything you have done so far. The meeting is now closed."

Bill's withered left arm was aching quite badly, as he left the meeting accompanied by Gillian. It didn't, however, detract from his overall satisfaction at how progress was being made. He was feeling so good that he invited Gillian out for a meal, hoping that with any luck she may even come back to his Surbiton flat and stay the night again.

Chapter 19 – Gang justice had been done

Dawn was breaking as Bill quietly eased his hot, sweaty, naked body out of the bed, being careful not to wake the beautiful young woman who had shared it with him all night. Usually, he wouldn't lie in bed a moment longer than was necessary. As soon as he woke, he got up, but this morning it wasn't so easy. Their night of all-consuming passion was so wonderful that it had even made him forget his physical deformity. His withered arm had caused him so much anguish throughout his life, but not last night. The woman was neither awake nor in a deep sleep. During this in-between state, dreams ran rampant through her subconscious. Cradling the pillow tighter to her chest, a small groan of satisfaction escaped from her full rounded lips. *What a night, I've never experienced such passion in all my life*, he thought as he picked up his clothes from where they lay on the floor. It may have been his imagination, but he seemed to feel a strong sexual magnetism emanating from her soft body trying to pull him back to bed. He ached for her and although sorely tempted to stay, he couldn't. Before leaving the bedroom, he stole a few minutes to gaze down at the shapely form just visible in the darkness. Bending down he kissed her gently on the forehead. Gillian never stirred. The bedroom silence was broken only by the soft sound of her gentle breathing.

Disappointed at having to leave, he consoled himself with his belief that business was far more important than lovemaking. This was especially true when vast sums of money were at stake. James Martindale was due to leave his five star hotel "The Brittania", to return to Scotland later in the morning. Bill needed to implement another part of his strategy, to divert some of the Gold from *HMS Sussex*; therefore he had arranged a breakfast meeting with him at 8.30am. James would become an unwitting accomplice in Bill's great master plan, if he handled it right. Although James's company, AB Salvage, was part of the business empire owned by the criminal mastermind, Craig Burke, it was run on a purely legitimate basis. Bill had been warned not to let the Managing Director of AB Salvage get even a hint that anything underhand was going on. Although Craig ran all his activities from a Scottish Hebridean Island, the tentacles of his organisation stretched far and wide. He could punish failure anywhere in the world. Bill Wyman had to tread very carefully.

"I'll have an omelette with some bacon and mushrooms," James responded to the waiter's request for their breakfast order.

"Can I have the Eggs Benedict?" Bill requested.

"I'm sure you won't be disappointed Sir, as it is one of Chef's specialities."

When the waiter had gone James poured out their coffee. This had been served to them as they took their place at the white clothed breakfast table, with the sparkling crystal glasses and silver cutlery. The exquisitely designed, ultra-modern, hotel restaurant boasted high ceilings making the room very light and airy. It gave a feeling of peace and calm, and was therefore extremely conducive to their planning meeting.

"This coffee is good," James said as he savoured his first mouthful. Then anxious to find out why Bill wanted he asked, "What was it that you wanted to discuss with me?"

"I know that your Head of Operations and my Assistant are going out to Andalucia. I know you have already given instructions to your man there to get the preparations underway. Security will be a tremendously important factor in ensuring the success of Project Sussex. In fact, it is so important an issue that I feel full responsibility can't be left to the team on the ground." Bill paused to have another drink of the delicious coffee.

"I have absolute faith and trust in Tom Dickson," James replied with a bit of an edge to his tone as he thought Bill was being critical of his friend. "I know that he will do a good job."

"Don't misunderstand me. I have no doubt that he will do a good job, and that he will work well with the other members of the team when they arrive in Spain. The only question I have is that does he have any contacts with good reliable, efficient, security companies as we will need to employ a bit of muscle? We will need well trained and experienced personnel, capable of dealing with armed attackers, to guard our storage of equipment and other requirements. They will also be essential if we are successful in landing any of the gold," Bill said.

"Sorry, I shouldn't have snapped like that. What do you suggest?"

"I have contacts in this area and can arrange for four security specialists to fly out to join the team," Bill responded. *This is going well*, he thought to himself.

James had a habit of focussing on a distant object, and staring at it, when giving consideration to anything of importance. The light drumming of his fingers on the table was another sign that he was deep in thought. "Who would the four security guards report to?" said James, breaking the silence.

"I suggest they report to your Tom Dickson, as he is the one who is to arrange the storage facilities and supplies of food and material." Bill knew that James would like this proposition of giving his friend a greater degree of involvement. Bill was lying. The guards would act as if they reported to Tom, but in reality they would only take orders from him. Another secret Bill withheld from James was the fact the four guards were not employed by an official security company, they were enforcers who worked for Craig Burke. This had already been agreed between Craig Burke and Bill. They both wanted their own people on hand who would have no compulsion in using force, even killing if necessary, to protect their interests.

"Ok, I agree. It makes sense. Can I leave you to make the necessary arrangements?" James said.

"Yes, I'll deal with everything and keep you updated." Bill went along with the deceit but he had no intention of keeping his word.

* * *

The powerful engines of the Broadblue 435s2 were cut to allow the catamaran to slowly float to its moorings. As his boat gently bumped against the moorings, Tom Dickson lent over the side to secure it. He had been very busy over the last few weeks, getting everything in place for the arrival of the *MV Staffa*, an Ocean Research Vessel, which his friend was sending. A full explanation for this had never been given, so he was still very much in the dark. It didn't matter to him however, as he saw it as a chance to repay his friend for saving his life all those years ago. He knew all would be revealed in the fullness of time.

Earlier in the day he had sailed his boat to one of his favourite spots to do some fishing and scuba diving. It had been a great day. Having solved his biggest problem, this day of relaxation was his reward. He had been instructed to rent a warehouse, or some other sort of storage building, of about twenty-five thousand square feet in area. He had spent weeks looking, but to no avail. Just two days previously however, he had come across a new letting which had recently been released to the market. It was a very old storage unit, quite dilapidated and a little smaller than the size specified. It was located half way between his Villa and Estapona, a small traditional fishing port where the group, from AB Salvage, could relax when they were not on duty. Believing that it would be ideal, he immediately contacted the letting agents, agreed a price and period of let, and briefed his lawyer. It was now down to the legal people to sort out the paperwork but he had achieved what was asked of him. He was happy and looking forward to the forthcoming adventure.

* * *

On "Eagle Island," the very overcast early morning sky didn't bode well for the many bird watchers who had come to the island especially to catch glimpses of white-tailed sea eagles, seeking their prey. Residents on the Isle of Mull were quite proud of the nickname "Eagle Island," as it helped to attract many visitors and thus boost the local economy. As the morning progressed the sun's rays shone down on the beautiful island and warmed the mountains and glens. The overcast sky soon gave way to a clear, sunny blue sky. It was ideal conditions for the white-tailed sea eagles. It seemed as if the entire island population of these special, wonderful birds were on display. Some glided effortlessly allowing the air thermals to do most of the work. It seemed as if others were playing chase as they raced through the sky. It was a wonderful sight.

"Wonderful, just wonderful," the man watching the amazing display, through his powerful Pentax binoculars, whispered. He had a fantastic vantage point on his Lochbuie Castle bedroom balcony. He enjoyed every minute that his busy schedule would allow, observing his favourite birds in flight. Craig Burke loved these birds so much, that he even had a sea eagle tattooed onto his right arm. Craig was a Jekyll and Hyde type of character. He could be exceedingly generous, and donated a great deal of money to protect the island's natural habitat. He was also extremely active in matters of bird conservation. On the other hand, he could be ruthless in business matters and would have no hesitation in having anyone injured or killed if they were either causing him, or his organisation, a problem.

Lowering his binoculars, he turned to see who had opened the sliding glass door from his bedroom.

"Good morning, John. Isn't this a great sight?" he said pointing to the sea eagles.

John Woodward didn't have the same appreciation as his employer. Always the diplomat, especially when it came to creating the right impression, he said, "Yes, boss, they are amazing and beautiful birds."

"I don't suppose you've come to see the eagles, so what have you to report?" Craig said to his right hand man.

"I've been dealing with the issue caused by the ambush on our gun shipment at Baardhere in Somalia. Chris Tennant had a suspicion that it was one of his men who informed the Government Troops. We agreed that I should send two of our people to make the necessary enquiries. Chis, was the only other person who knew the identities of the two enforcers and he provided them with everything they needed. They followed up some rumours regarding one person in particular, who worked at the warehouse at Baardhere. It seems that he boasted about the sudden settling of his considerable debts, but nobody could work out where the money came from. He certainly couldn't have saved the amount involved from his pay. Without going into great detail, I can tell you, that after our people interviewed him, he confessed and the matter is now closed." John didn't elaborate on the fact that the informer suffered a great deal of pain during the interview process. His mutilated and decapitated body had been buried in the desert. Gang justice had been done.

Craig Burke showed no emotion or concern when he heard this update. He simply registered the facts. "Now tell me the latest news about The Sussex Project. Has it resumed since the delay caused by the fire at the shipyard?" he enquired.

"Yes, the project, is now back on track. I have sent the four men, requested by Bill, to Estapona. They are our best and are very efficient and reliable. Bill has managed to get James Martindale to agree to their secondment, without letting him suspect the real reason for them to be included in their operational team," John replied.

"Good, now will you join me for dinner? Over dinner, we will discuss how we can replace the gun shipment that was unfortunately stopped from getting to Baardhere."

Chapter 20 – The summons to the Foreign Office

"LOOK OUT! WATCH WHAT YOU'RE DOING! Tom snapped at the man unloading the delivery vehicle. The warning came too late. The large weighty cylindrical oxygen tank careered from the vehicle and crashed, with an almighty thud, onto the yard. Fernando, who had been kneeling beside some of the wooden cases filled with canned provisions, made his escape with just inches to spare, as the heavy torpedo shaped canister rolled towards him. "Because of your carelessness someone could have been killed!" Tom was usually a mild mannered man, but he always got riled when people didn't take proper due care and failed to pay attention when dealing with heavy or dangerous objects. *Why is it that no one seems to care about Health and Safety nowadays?* The question which flashed through his mind was one to which he was unable to supply an answer. "Forgive me!" Stuttered the delivery man as he offered his rather feeble apology. The tank slipped and I couldn't catch it in time."

"I should think so! You could've killed someone!" Tom was also mindful of the high cost of such equipment. "If you are to make any more deliveries here, you need to buck your ideas up, or you could find yourself having to pay for any damage," Tom retorted. Other than this unfortunate incident Tom was pleased with the way matters had been progressing.

Catching sight of Juan, the Supervisor he had hired to manage the receipt and storage of deliveries to the warehouse, he walked up to him to get an update. The short swarthy man with the round jovial face, turned towards Tom as he approached. His face was beaming and his huge smile seemed to illuminate his face. Juan loved his job; he was an efficient and meticulous type of guy. He liked everything to be in its proper place. It was important to him that stored items could be found easily. To make this happen he dashed through the warehouse from one end to another, then back again issuing orders and directions, remonstrating with staff if they put something in the wrong location. He was like a human whirlwind. Although Juan had never worked for Tom before, they had known each other for years and often met in La Regatta, at the Marina in Estapona, for a drink. Tom was glad that he had managed to employ him.

"Yes, Tom, everything is going well. Once the vehicle outside is unloaded the last of the deliveries will have been received," Juan said.

"That's good. Phone me later to let me know when everything has been stored and you have secured the warehouse. I have to return to my villa, rather sharpish as I have two guests arriving and I need to be home for them."

"Ok, I will do as you ask."

Tom had offered to meet his two guests at the airport, but they said they would hire a car and make their own way. As they had decided to fly to Malaga Airport, rather than Gibraltar International Airport which was a lot nearer, he was relieved that he didn't have to make the 126Km round trip. Arriving back at his Villa, Tom checked his watch. He had just over an hour and a half to do his final tidying up. *I'd better get a move on* he thought, as he went into the first of his two spare rooms. They were small and sparsely furnished, but his guests would be comfortable enough. There was a selfish motive behind his offer to provide accommodation for the people his friend James was sending out from England, rather than find lodging in Estapona. Communications would be so much easier if they were close to the harbour and the warehouse. Tom had spent so much time on his own he thought it a good opportunity to have some company; even if it was only for a short time.

The names of Gillian Young and Jim Wilson meant nothing to him and he knew very little about them. It was obvious that one was male and one was female. He did know however, that they were experts in the field

The Sussex Gold

of explorations and treasure hunting. Hopefully he would get to know more over the next few days.

"That was a great meal, Tom," Gillian said after drinking the last of her coffee.

"I agree," echoed Jim. "It has been a long day and we were both ready for it."

"I have some of the Hunter's, Pinot Noir left. Would you like to finish it off?" Tom enquired. Jim would have preferred a beer but just to be hospitable he shared the remainder of the bottle with Gillian.

After their meal Tom was brought up to speed with The Sussex Project. He learnt about the bribe that the British Government, in 1694, despatched to the Duke of Savoy, on board *HMS Sussex*. He learnt about the violent storm that caused *HMS Sussex* to sink off the coast of Gibraltar. Five hundred crew members were killed with only two surviving. "So the Duke never got the gold he was expecting?" Tom questioned.

"No, and more to the point neither did anyone else. The gold has never been retrieved and is still in the hold of the sunken *HMS Sussex*. This is why the British Government has instigated Project Sussex, they believe the gold is rightfully theirs and they want it back," Gillian said.

"Has there ever been any attempt to retrieve the gold before now?" Tom asked.

"No, because the shipwreck lies in water over half-a-mile deep; the necessary technology and equipment to reach it hasn't been available until recently. The gold and the ship still remain undisturbed," Gillian replied.

Jim was aware of the conversation but didn't play any part in it; he sat very quietly, stroking his salt and pepper beard. "You look deep in thought," Tom said.

"Sorry, I have just been wondering if our equipment will arrive as planned."

"Don't worry about it. I'm sure it will be fine. Earlier today, I spoke to the Managing Director of AB Salvage who assures me that everything is on schedule. He confirmed that the *MV Staffa* which is bringing all the underwater gear we need, including the remote, and the Deep Rovers etc. will arrive tomorrow." Gillian said.

"That's good. We'll need two days to test all the equipment and to brief the team on how we propose to deal with the search for *HMS Sussex*. I am so excited about this project and will be happy when we can get it underway," Jim replied.

"I was also told that the ship would be carrying four passengers who are to be responsible for all our security requirements. The strange thing about it is that the Managing Director told me that they were to report to you, Tom, on a day-to-day basis," Gillian continued.

"I know nothing about this."

"I've been informed that they will bring a letter for you explaining all the details."

"I'm not sure about this. I've never been responsible for security before, but I suppose I had better wait and see what the letter says," Tom said rather resignedly.

* * *

The Spanish Ambassador hated the English Weather, with a passion. Heavy downpours of rain, fog and ice were not conditions he was happy with. Francisco Moran Aguirre was born in the Aravaca suburb, in the North West of Madrid, spending the first twenty years of his life there until the completion of his education. Choosing to study for a degree, at the Universdad Complutense Madrid, he did well and obtained a First in Modern Languages and Literature. After completing his BA he undertook further studies and was rewarded with a Master's in Political

Analysis. He joined the Spanish Diplomatic Service as soon as there was a vacancy. This was a career choice that he had fostered since being a young teenager. Being very bright and astute he progressed rapidly until he reached the exalted position of Ambassador. Various postings took him to Africa and the Middle East. His longest appointments were the five years each he spent in Riyadh, Saudi Arabia and in Dubai, UAE. He was used, therefore, to much higher temperatures and greater sunshine. Despite the inclement weather, he loved his new recent transfer to London. His record had been faultless. Success and achievement had been his trade mark throughout his career. This so impressed his Government masters that the decision of who to send to London, when the incumbent ambassador retired, was an easy one. This promotion and appointment gave him a lot of personal satisfaction as it was something he had worked hard for, over many years, in the service of his country.

"Sir, take this umbrella," his chauffeur said, handing him one for protection against the drizzly shower of rain which had started ten minutes earlier.

Grasping the umbrella the Spanish Ambassador moved quickly from his official car to the Foreign Office. He entered through the special, King Charles Street, entrance reserved for senior diplomats of his status. "Good evening, Constable," he greeted the policeman who ushered him into the large reception room after checking his permit. Although just a reception room, Francisco Moran Aguirre was always impressed by how grand and ornate it was. Directly across from the entrance door was an excellent photograph of Her Majesty Queen Elizabeth. The photographer had done an outstanding job with the use of soft lighting and although this was a formal photograph he had captured the natural smile of his subject.

"Can I help you, Sir," the beautiful receptionist, with the long silky red hair and rather pompous voice asked. She was dressed very conventionally and her crisp blouse was whiter than white. No doubt this was to give an air of professionalism. Francisco didn't spoil the illusion by mentioning that he had noticed her rapidly hiding the tea cup under the desk when his permit was being checked.

"I have an appointment with the Foreign Secretary," he replied. There was no trace of a Spanish accent in his voice; he could speak fluent English as indeed he could with several other languages.

As the receptionist picked up the internal telephone to inform the Foreign Secretary of the Ambassadors arrival, he took a seat in one of the comfortable armchairs, from where he could view the wonderful works of art decorating the walls. Every time he waited in this room he was fascinated by the painting of "The Battle of Waterloo," by the British painter George Jones. He often wondered how the French Ambassador must feel when he too viewed the painting.

Sometimes, when he was summoned to the Foreign Office, he had to listen to some petty complaint relating to bad behaviour from one of his citizens, or His Government may have made some strategic decision that upset the British, but he had absolutely no idea why his presence was required this evening.

The shrill ringing interrupted his thoughts, "The Foreign Secretary will see you now and his assistant is on her way down to take you to him," the receptionist said, after answering the telephone.

Chapter 21 – The four passengers

William Fox had only been Foreign Secretary for just over a year although, to him, it felt much longer. There had been no honeymoon period, and right from the beginning he was immersed in sorting out a number of major politically sensitive issues. If not handled with some finesse and brought to a satisfactory conclusion, dire repercussions would be incurred. On top of everything else, he was working on a paper that the Prime Minister had asked him to produce. He was to review the second of the four main Foreign Policy Goals, and make any necessary recommendations for updating it. This was not an easy matter for him and his team, as the policy was very wide ranging, in that it covered the prevention and resolution of conflict.

Initially he wasn't pleased that his colleague, the Minister of Defence, had asked him to host a meeting between the Spanish Ambassador to London, and Joshua Campbell, the Under-Secretary for Defence. He felt that Defence Ministers should keep their noses out of foreign relation matters and stick to what they do best. He realised however, that Joshua had dual responsibilities as he was also Minister for International Security Strategy. Joshua was well known in the foreign office department and was highly regarded as an achiever. Perhaps it wasn't such a bad idea to let him get involved in the negotiations with the Spanish. As a senior member of the Cabinet he was very much aware of Project Sussex and of its importance to the Government. He also knew that any discussions would not be easy, and anyway he had a full work load so time was of the essence.

Joshua was already in his office when his assistant brought the Spanish Ambassador from the reception room. He formally introduced Joshua to Francisco Moran Aguirre, and then gave a brief synopsis of why the meeting was called. "Before the two of you start talking, would you care for a glass of this fine red wine, it is an Alion Reserva, Vega Sicilia?"

"I see you have chosen a Spanish wine. If I had been the French Ambassador would you have offered a French wine instead?" Francisco said with the faintest hint of a smile.

I can see the Ambassador is going to be a little touchy, thought Joshua.

"No, I just really like it and would highly recommend it to anyone," the Foreign Secretary replied as he poured out a healthy measure into each of the crystal wine glasses.

Clutching their glasses of wine, the three moved to the comfortable armchairs situated in the less formal part of the Foreign Secretary's office. William believed that more could be achieved when participants were able to discuss matters in a relaxed atmosphere. He knew that meetings around a boardroom table were needed for larger groups, but could inhibit free flowing discussion with smaller groups.

"Now Joshua, tell me, what is it that you want from the Spanish Government?" Francisco enquired as he settled into his armchair. Having heard the synopsis he was anxious to get straight into the detail of what the Under-Secretary for Defence wanted.

During the next hour Joshua went into a lot more detail about what the Government wanted to achieve with Project Sussex. He explained the desire of the British Government to salvage its property, unfortunately sunk in sixteen hundred and ninety four. He explained about the need to honour the requirements of the various archaeological groups, if the *HMS Sussex* shipwreck was found. He confirmed that the British Government was mindful of its international agreements, and the necessity to comply with Maritime Law. He emphasised that the Government wanted to ensure that the pursuit of their objective, didn't damage relations with Spain.

Although Joshua was very polite and diplomatic in his discussions with Francisco, he left him in no doubt that *HMS Sussex*, with all its contents belonged to the British Government and they had a right to get it back. Neither the Foreign Secretary, nor Joshua however, had been completely honest with the Spanish Ambassador. They had deliberately withheld the fact that the holds of the shipwrecked *HMS Sussex*, were still full of gold coins worth a King's Ransom. Both the British Government representatives knew that eventually, as a point of negotiation, they would need to reveal the real reason for embarking on a search for this shipwreck. For the present however, they thought it best to keep it a secret.

"Thank you for informing me about your desire regarding *HMS Sussex*, but obviously I have to communicate with my Government for a decision, before you can proceed with your search in Spanish waters. I will get back to you as soon as I am able," Francisco said as he rose from his armchair. Once again Joshua wasn't open about the fact that he knew an Ocean Class Research Ship was already well on its way to the coast of Andalucia, Spain.

"We would be grateful for an early reply as there is a lot to organise," Joshua said.

"As it's late, my staff will have gone home for the evening, so I'll show you out," the Foreign Secretary said to Francisco. "Joshua, can you stay as I need some information from you for a meeting tomorrow? As soon as I have let Francisco out, I'll come straight back."

Joshua didn't have to wait long for William to get back. "How do you think that went?" Joshua asked.

"Honestly? I think he knows we are not putting all our cards on the table. I think we're going to have some difficulties."

"We'll just have to wait and see, but in the meantime the Project will proceed as planned," Joshua said.

* * *

The Research Ship had made good progress, arriving at its destination two hours earlier than anticipated. The *MV Staffa* would act as the "mother ship," in support of the deep sea submersibles that were to be used in the search for the shipwreck. Tom Dickson was amazed when he saw it at anchor in the same natural harbour he moored his Catamaran. Turning to Gillian and Jim, who stood beside him on the beachfront of his villa, "I've not seen a ship like that before."

"I'm very proud of her and have carried out many explorations on her; she is so reliable and carries every piece of equipment you could possibly need to search for shipwrecks. She carries two Deep Rovers and a dual Deep Worker, as well as all the other equipment we'll need," Jim answered.

Gillian had made no attempt to reply for she was already speaking on her mobile. Gillian was a music lover. Her taste was wide ranging as long as the music had a good beat, with the music of Scott Joplin being a particular favourite. Therefore, she had set the ringtone on her mobile to "The Entertainer."

It was obvious how proud Jim was of the *MV Staffa*, but before he could continue Tom interrupted him, "I don't understand what you mean!"

"Once we get on board I'll give you a tour, and explain everything to you in as much detail as you want. But in simple terms the Deep Rovers and Dual Deep Worker are deep sea submersibles that allow imaging and sampling to be carried out at depths of three thousand two hundred and eighty feet. This depth rating gives them access to forty percent of the world's oceans. The "mother ship", as I call the *MV Staffa*, has three upper decks which are furnished to a level of comfort rarely seen on exploration ships. She has six first class cabins, exceptional lounge and dining facilities. She has fourteen crew members and six submersible team members. Fourteen to twenty other passengers can be accommodated if required. Once you get to see her up close, you'll understand why I enjoy working on her."

Jim knew all the members of the crew and submersible team personally. Over the years they had shared numerous experiences, many of them life threatening, and as a result he had forged a close understanding with each of them.

After replacing her mobile into the special case, which clipped onto the belt of her blue denim jeans, Gillian informed them that the Captain was sending his small tender to pick them up from the jetty, in an hour's time.

"Good to meet you again, Jim," the Captain of the *MV Staffa* greeted him as he came on board the ship with Tom and Gillian. Jim felt as if his arm was going to be torn from his shoulder, when the Captain shook his hand in a powerful vice like grip. Jim had momentarily forgotten how strong his colleague and friend was. Before Jim could reply the Captain turned to face Gillian, "So this is the lovely lady I spoke to on the phone earlier?"

"Yes, Captain, I'm pleased to meet you."

"We don't stand on ceremony here, my girl. My name is Karl and I would prefer we stick to first names," his beaming smile softened the rather curt retort.

"That's fine by me, Captain, sorry I mean Karl. Can I introduce you to Tom who will also be working with us on this project?"

After all the introductions were over they moved to the ships comfortable lounge, where Karl had arranged for some light refreshment to be provided. Jim and Karl had so much catching up to do that for the first twenty minutes or so, both Tom and Gillian were excluded from the conversation. Normally Tom wouldn't have minded, but he was rather fidgety and anxious to meet the four mysterious passengers who were to hand him a letter of instruction. He couldn't wait any longer so he said, "I apologise for interrupting, but I understand that you have four passengers who have something for me."

"Yes, of course I will ask them to join us. You must excuse us; we didn't mean to be rude."

It was only five minutes until Karl returned to the lounge with the four passengers. They were an imposing group. They all wore black paramilitary type clothing with heavy boots. Tom's knowledge of what a security guard looks like was rather limited, but these guys didn't fit his mental picture. They looked alert and dangerous. They looked well trained and professional. They looked ex-military.

Chapter 22 – ROV launched

Dear Tom,

By now you will have met Jack McDonald and his security team. The Management Committee, responsible for the overall planning for Project Sussex have decided that it is necessary to take this precaution. There is too much at stake to leave security matters in the hands of personnel who have no track record with us. Jack McDonald is known to one of my senior colleagues on the Management Committee and he convinced us that he is the best man for the job.

I am aware that you don't have any specialist knowledge in this field, therefore all security planning and decision making will be his sole responsibility. For all other matters he is to report directly to you. Jack is aware of this arrangement and has voiced no objections. The MV Staffa has been loaded with all the equipment and resources they need, so there will be no need for you to be involved in making any purchases on their behalf.

Well, my friend, I know that this may seem as if we are taking a liberty in giving you this added responsibility. I assure you however, that we would not have sanctioned this if we felt that it wasn't absolutely necessary. I know that you will participate fully with this requirement.

I would like to take this opportunity to "Thank you" for what you have done so far, and also to wish you every success as you play your part in helping to recover the gold that belongs to our country.

James Martindale.
Managing Director
AB Salvage.

So this is what it means to "go the extra mile", Tom pondered as he carefully folded the letter. When he was a young man his father had always applied this principle to everything he did by doing more than was expected from him. Tom's father believed this was a major factor in his business success. Whenever he could, Tom tried to follow his father's example but this request may just be too much. He slipped the letter into the hip pocket of his jeans so he could re-read it later.

Jack's team went to their quarters, whilst Tom spent the next hour briefing him on the main locations requiring his attention. The *MV Staffa* would obviously be a high security priority, followed by Tom's villa and the warehouse which Tom had recently rented. Jack bombarded Tom with a host of questions helping him build up a mental picture of access roads, layouts of the villa and warehouse, key holders etc. When the briefing was complete Tom realised Jack was an expert in his chosen field, and really knew his stuff. However, he wasn't an easy man to take a liking to. He seemed distant, cold and calculating. He was very sullen and had a high degree of self confidence. There was something unexplainable about Jack's demeanour that made Tom very uneasy.

It was very late when Tom, Gillian and Jim Wilson left the Research Ship to make their way back to Tom's Villa. It had taken some effort for Gillian to prise Jim away from his "toys." He gave particular attention to the remote controlled submersible with its 25-mile-long remote fibre optic cable. He wanted to ensure that the cable, specialised cameras and sonar units which had been destroyed or damaged by the fire back at the Greenock Shipyard, had been fully replaced. Gillian had felt surplus to requirements when Jim abandoned her to check the equipment.

"Are you happy now?" she said with a tone of frustration and exasperation, when she went to inform him Tom was ready to return to the villa. She realised how important it was to verify that all the equipment was in working order, but she had so wanted Jim to include her in the process.

* * *

"That was a great breakfast," Tom said to Gillian as he devoured the last mouthful of his bacon and eggs.

"Yes, it was really good and a hot strong mug of coffee would just finish it off," Jim Wilson said.

"Well you know where the kettle is. Make coffee for the three of us and I'll deal with the dirty dishes," Gillian replied.

Jim reluctantly put the kettle on. He was a male chauvinist at heart and didn't think it was man's work to make coffee. Gillian overhead him muttering under his breath, "Is there a problem, Jim?" she asked.

"No, no, everything is fine," he grunted.

As they sat down at the table to drink their coffee, Tom informed them Jack McDonald would be bringing one of his men over to the villa, later in the morning.

"What's that all about?" Gillian wanted to know.

"He wants him to inspect the villa and then wishes to visit the warehouse. I understand there is a plan for the security guard to patrol both locations and he will be relieved from time to time by one of his colleagues. I also believe one of the team will be kept permanently on the *MV Staffa* whilst Jack McDonald is to perform a floating role, if you'll pardon the pun. It looks like I am going to be busy all morning chauffeuring these two about," Tom replied.

"While you are doing that, Gillian and I will return to the Research Ship and make plans for making our exploratory searches with the remotely controlled submersible," Jim said with a touch of excitement in his voice. Being a "hands on" person he couldn't wait to get involved with the more practical aspects of the operation.

Jim knew that even though the area of the Mediterranean where their search for *HMS Sussex* was to be focussed, was not as deep as the Mariana Trench, the deepest part of the ocean, it would bring its own challenges. The development of submersibles has come a long way since the Swiss underwater explorer; Auguste Piccard created, together with a shipyard, the first submersible which actually worked on a professional level. He was happy therefore, that the deep-sea submersibles, both remotely controlled and manned, which were available to him, were in a different class. Advanced technologies had continuously virtually opened the water deeper and deeper.

On arriving back on board the *MV Staffa* they headed directly for the Dive Control Centre. All surface support ships possessed such centres to manage the operation of their marine robots. "Morning team," Jim said to the two people already present in the centre. The room was tightly packed with Computers, scanners of various types, sonic detectors, radio equipment, as well as many other associated pieces of equipment. The numerous screens were boringly blank and lifeless. In a short time they would spring into life with their screens being illuminated with various colourful images. "Right, let's get the show on the road."

* * *

The mother ship was a hive of activity and excitement as preparations were made for the launch of the ROV. The prime objective, for the Remotely Operated Vehicle was to pinpoint the exact location of *HMS Sussex*, so that they could then put the Deep Rovers and the Dual Deep Worker to good use.

Various deck winches made a terrible clanging din as the deckhands put them to work. The umbilical winch was of particular importance and required to be carefully handled. This winch was fitted with a special mechanism to ensure even spooling of the umbilical cable which connected the ROV to the mother ship. Other deckhands operated the twenty-three tonne "A" frame, with its elevated pivot point to allow clearance of the ROV as it was lifted over the ship's side. Gillian grabbed Jim's arm in excitement as the ROV slid beneath the waves, "There it goes!"

Although Jim Wilson, in his capacity as Head of Explorations for AB Salvage Limited, had been involved with many similar launches, he too felt exhilarated as if it was his first time. He pulled his chair closer to the Dive Control monitors to get a better view of the video images, and data signals, coming back from the submerged ROV being driven to the sea floor by its powerful thrusters. The ROV LED lights had a range of some ten feet ahead of the submerged vehicle, but nothing of interest was yet being transmitted. Jim had warned Gillian not to expect quick results as in his experience, such investigations always took far longer than expected. Settling more comfortably into his chair he prepared himself for a long day.

"Well, today has been a complete waste of time," Gillian said disappointedly. Despite the warning not to expect quick results she had really felt that the wreck site would have been found. "I really felt that we would have discovered her today. I know that her last reported position may not have been a hundred percent accurate, but we surveyed a reasonable area around that position."

"It doesn't always work like that," Jim responded. "Sometimes it can take weeks or months before any wreckage, or artefacts from the targeted shipwreck are discovered. The sea is very effective at hiding anything committed to its depths. We need to have a lot of patience together with methodically performing a systematic and controlled search pattern."

"I know, I know. I do understand. Sorry for being so impatient."

"Look, let's retrieve the ROV and call it a day. We'll resume the search tomorrow. You never know, we may be lucky."

Chapter 23 – The Spanish Ambassador's Bombshell

Joshua Campbell decided to *"beard the lion in its den"*, by meeting the Spanish Ambassador in his own environment. Two days had elapsed since Francisco Moran Aguirre had contacted him to arrange a meeting to discuss a matter of mutual importance. The diplomat, always the consummate professional, didn't give anything away despite Joshua's attempts to get him to divulge the subject matter.

Joshua was normally a very patient man but traffic congestion in London always frustrated him. Travelling anywhere in the metropolis always took far longer than was necessary. He consoled himself with the fact that the situation was not as bad as it would be if he lived in Mumbai, India. Joshua had recently been to this business capital of India, one of the most populated cities in the world. It is home to more than 20.4 million people and he had never experienced such absolute chaos, in a city centre. Traffic control police exercised no control whatsoever, causing gridlock on a daily basis. The vehicles disgorged their occupants who shouted loudly and gesticulated widely, but this never made any immediate effect to the huge traffic jams.

As his driver guided the Government car through the heavy London traffic, he pressed the Green answer button to silence the loud ringing of his mobile telephone. Although Joshua thought that the mobile telephone was one of the great inventions he also felt it could be so intrusive. There was nowhere to hide from its reach. Glancing at the display he saw the caller was William Fox.

"Good morning, Foreign Secretary."

"Morning, Joshua. I got your message. Are you on your way to meet Francisco?"

"Yes, I should arrive there in about ten minutes."

"Have you managed to find out what he wants to see you about?"

"No, I think I'll just have to wait until I get to his office," Joshua said.

"Ok, but be careful he doesn't trick you into saying something that we may later regret."

"Don't worry, Sir, I'll be careful." Joshua was used to participating in high level discussions and was rather annoyed by what he felt was an unnecessary caution.

A few minutes later the car arrived at Belgrave Square, the centre piece of Belgravia, one of the grandest and largest nineteenth century squares in London. As Joshua's car approached the Spanish Embassy gates he saw hundreds of protestors who had gathered outside, supporting calls for a real democracy and a new constitution for Spain. The demonstration was peaceful and the car was not prevented from gaining access to the embassy compound. After a slightly frosty welcome from the Spanish Ambassador, with no time being wasted in pleasantries, they got straight down to business.

"I have given careful consideration to the request you made at our last meeting. I need to inform you I am going to recommend, to my Government, that all operations, regarding Project Sussex, be suspended for the foreseeable future." Following the notification from the British Governments regarding their Project Sussex, he had carried out his own research. He was now aware of the full facts. He knew about the secret mission and where *HMS Sussex* was headed when it was unfortunately sunk. He knew about the gold. He didn't know, however, that the search for *HMS Sussex* had already begun.

Oh, my God! I hope Francisco doesn't know about the MV Staffa, Joshua wondered. "Why would you do that? The British Government has a right to seek to get back what belongs to it," he retorted rather angrily. Joshua wasn't sure what to expect from the Ambassador but he certainly didn't expect such a direct confrontation.

"The ship lies in Spanish waters; therefore, we have a right to set some conditions. Included in my recommendation is a suggestion for the regional government of Andalusia to appoint an expert to observe operations on the wreck site. I feel more time is needed to review the archaeological plan which your Government has submitted. Care needs to be taken so that this project doesn't turn into nothing more than a treasure hunt." The Ambassador stopped short of making Joshua aware he had discovered the secret of the *Sussex*. He knew about the cargo of tons of gold coins which sank with the ship.

"Is there nothing we can do to help you make a more positive recommendation?"

"I'm afraid not for I need to ensure that Spain's interests are protected," the Ambassador replied.

"The British Government has gone to a great deal of expense and has made several commitments which can't be cancelled overnight. If we are required to suspend operations we need some time to make the necessary arrangements."

"I can see your point. As a gesture of goodwill I will suggest the suspension of operations becomes effective four weeks from the date of my report. That should give you enough time to put matters in hand."

"If that's the best you can do I will inform my Government and wait to hear the response from yours."

"Well I think our business is now concluded. I'll get my secretary to show you out and I'll be in touch as soon as possible."

Joshua wasn't a violent man but, just at that moment, he could easily have punched the Spanish Ambassador on the nose. If he had known the Ambassador had found out that Joshua and William Fox had deliberately withheld the information concerning the gold, he would have understood why he wasn't received with open arms. No one likes being lied to.

Back in Andalusia Jim Wilson and the onsite operational team were completely in the dark about these unsuccessful talks. Their search for the sunken treasure ship continued.

* * *

Davy Alexander was so angry on hearing Joshua Campbell's update of the outcome of his meeting with the Spanish Ambassador, "Damn! Damn! Damn! This is not good news. Is he really serious about carrying out his threat and scuppering Project Sussex?"

"Yes, I'm afraid I believe he will do exactly as he said." Joshua replied without any hesitation, for he had no doubt of Francisco Moran Aguirre's determination.

"We need to get the team together, as soon as possible, to discuss this latest development. Can you get Bill Wyman to be here by 2.00pm this afternoon, and I will arrange for a conference call to be set up with James Martindale, to enable him to take part from his company office in Greenock?

Once the arrangements for the emergency meeting were made Davy Alexander had some free time, which he used to catch up on his research of some of the shipwrecks that salvagers would most love to find. This was a subject he had not previously been interested in, but his involvement with Project Sussex had whetted his appetite.

Notre Dame de Deliverance: Chartered by Spain to return treasures from South America, this French West Indies merchant ship was carrying 500kg (1100lb) of gold bullion, 15,000 gold doubloons, six chests of gems, and more than a million silver pieces when she went down in a hurricane off Key West in 1755.

Merchant Royal: Once known as the 'Eldorado of the Seas', the treasure-laden vessel went down in a storm near the Isles of Scilly, off the south west coast of Britain, in 1641. The gold, silver and jewels concealed in the wreck are said to be worth more than $300 million. Some experts think the 'Black Swan' might be the *Merchant Royal*.

Grosvenor: Said to be the richest vessel ever lost by the British East India Company, *Grosvenor* sank off the eastern coast of South Africa in 1782. She was carrying 2.6 million gold coins, 1400 gold ingots and 19 chests of gems, as well as a jewel-encrusted gold throne from India.

The Admiral Nakhimov: Scuttled after being hit by a torpedo in the straits between Korea and Japan, this ship sank in 1905 during the Russian-Japanese War. She was said to have been carrying the entire fleet's pay, which amounted to 5000 boxes of gold coins, 48 gold ingots and 16 platinum ingots.

Flora del Mar: Carrying treasures taken from the then kingdom of Malacca, now part of Malaysia, the Portuguese ship went down off the northern coast of Sumatra in 1511. The cargo is said to include gold, diamonds, emeralds, and rubies.

Although developing an interest in such shipwrecks Davy knew that the Sussex Project would be the nearest that he would ever get to searching for sunken treasure. He had just completed reading the summary of the top five sunken treasure ships, when his attention was forced back to more immediate concerns regarding *HMS Sussex*. Sarah, his personal assistant interrupted his thoughts by contacting him on his private intercom, "Bill Wyman and Joshua Campbell have arrived, Minister, and I have established the telephone link with James Martindale."

"James please let me know if you have any problems with the telephone connection," Davy said as the meeting got under way. "Well gentlemen we have a problem. Joshua will brief you on his recent meeting with the Spanish Ambassador regarding our plans to retrieve the gold from *HMS*

Sussex which sank in Spanish Territorial waters." It didn't take very long for Joshua to impart a feeling of gloom and despondency as he unveiled the outcome of the discussions with Francisco Moran Aguirre.

"Are the Spanish aware that we have a ship currently conducting a search for the wreck even as we speak," James's voice was as clear as a bell, despite it being broadcast over the telephone loudspeaker.

"Not yet, as far as I am aware," Joshua replied. "We have managed to buy a bit of time as the Ambassador won't ask for any action, to be taken, until four weeks from the date of his report."

Bill Wyman's hands became very clammy and he started to perspire on hearing this terrible news. He had made promises. He had made promises to dangerous people and if they weren't kept he would suffer dire consequences. It was a critical situation, for him personally, so he had to do everything in his power to keep the project running. "If we've four weeks before the project is forced to be postponed can we keep focussed on the project until then? It might be possible to find the site, what does everyone think?"

"I can instruct Jim Wilson and his team, in Andalucía, to pull out all the stops in speeding up the search operation. Obviously I can't guarantee we'll find the site, in the time available, but we'll do our best." James said.

"We will need to be very careful how we handle this very delicate situation. I authorise you to keep the project moving forward as quickly as possible, but Joshua you need to keep in communication with the Spanish Ambassador and make sure he doesn't get wind of what we are doing. Bill you need to maintain your discussions with the various British archaeological societies without letting them know we have an issue. As this matter could affect our International relation with another member of the European Community, I will discuss this latest development with our Foreign Secretary."

After the meeting was drawn to a close and everyone went their separate ways, Bill Wyman felt that he should play safe and notify Craig Burke.

He wasn't afraid to pass bad news on to the criminal mastermind, he was terrified. Sometimes Craig over reacted to bad news, and may want to punish him even although he wasn't the instigator of the problem. Plucking up the courage he used the special telephone, which encrypted all messages, and dialled Craig's number. "I need to come and see you urgently," he said when the phone was answered.

Chapter 24 – The proposed bribe

Over many years Craig Burke had dealt with people from the full strata of society including the rich and powerful, as well as the dregs of humanity. His varied experiences had helped him to develop an ability to see beyond the words that people uttered. He could tell if he was being lied to or if the person speaking to him was hiding concerns or secrets. Immediately picking up the urgency in Bill Wyman's voice he responded accordingly. "I keep a private helicopter based at the London Heliport in Lombard Road on the Battersea Riverside. I'll instruct my pilot to have it ready for take-off within the next hour. Get there as quickly as possible and he'll fly you to the castle. Once you get to the Heliport make your way to Lochbuie Services and ask for Pete. When you introduce yourself he will ask for a password, which will be "Eagle Island."

Bill had never been in a helicopter before and didn't really relish the thought of it, but knew it was futile to try to get Craig Burke to change his mind. "As there are meetings for me to organise to maintain the pretence of assisting the British Government with Project Sussex, I'll need to return to London as soon as possible after I've updated you on the current situation."

"That's fine; I'll be waiting for you at Lochbuie Castle."

Shortly after their conversation ended Bill quickly changed out of his formal clothing, which he had worn for the recent meeting with the Defence Minister. Something more comfortable would be required for his helicopter flight to Scotland. He was soon behind the wheel of his high performance and luxurious Jaguar XKR. The highly advanced 5.0 litre V8 GEN III R supercharged engine gave him a thrill every time he switched on the ignition. Twenty-five minutes after leaving his flat in Surbiton he arrived at his destination. After parking his car in the secure customer parking area he went to find Pete.

Soon after Pete had confirmed he was the expected passenger they made their way to the sleek helicopter standing on the tarmac. They both climbed into the machine beautifully adorned in the bright blue and white colours of Lochbuie Services. Bill took the seat next to the pilot and listened, with some apprehension, as he made radio contact with Air Traffic Control. His stomach began to feel a little queasy, as the time for "takeoff" loomed nearer. He wasn't looking forward to this flight and would be glad when it was all over.

As the Bell Long Ranger Helicopter lifted off the ground, his feeling of sickness got worse. Both he and the pilot were seated in a comfortable leather interior and the advanced drive train system, developed for the Long Ranger, provided an unsurpassed incredibly smooth ride. He was, however, subjected to a fair amount of noise, generated from the main and tail rotor systems, despite the use of ear protectors. The general noise level was increased by the mechanical revolving systems attached to the rotors. Overall the in flight noise was nowhere near as bad as he had envisaged. As the flight progressed these factors helped him to relax, and he started to quite enjoy his new experience.

About two miles from Lochbuie Castle the helicopter descended to nine hundred feet above ground level. The Pilot slowed the ground speed from cruising speed to eighty knots, and then set the helicopter into a gradual descent of five hundred feet per minute, one mile from the landing zone. Bill was fascinated with the apparent ease which the pilot handled the various levers, sticks and pedals controlling the glide angle of the helicopter. One hundred yards from the landing zone, the helicopter's ground speed was dropped to twenty knots. Pete manipulated his controls to further reduce speed to ten knots, fifty yards from the landing zone. He then put the helicopter into a hover when it was three feet directly above the landing area. Bill was so relieved when the helicopter was gently lowered to the ground. He had arrived. He was safe.

The Sussex Gold

The engine was still running when Bill got out of the helicopter. With the airflow being pushed vertically downwards, by the spinning blades, he instinctively ducked his head as he moved away from his new mode of transport. When he was able to stand erect he spotted John Woodward waiting to meet him. The castle was only a short walk from the landing site, and very soon he would, once again, be face to face with one of the most powerful criminal masterminds in the country.

* * *

"Here, have a glass of my favourite seventeen year old single malt whisky, while you tell me what's so important you had to fly up here to see me," Craig said as he filled their glasses from an absolutely stunning crystal antique whisky decanter.

Bill was very fond of a glass of whisky, but had never tasted this special brew from the Bowmore Distillery on the Isle of Islay. "Very palatable, very palatable indeed," he said as the smooth liquid made him feel good.

It didn't take long to bring Craig up to speed with recent developments, especially the problem being caused by the Spanish Ambassador. When he had finished neither Craig nor John Woodward, his right hand man, gave any response for what seemed an eternity. It was John Woodward who first broke the silence. "I know how to stop this! I could arrange for this Ambassador to meet with a fatal accident!"

Before he could elaborate on his proposed solution, to this hiccup in the plans for getting their hands on some of the Sussex gold, Craig interrupted him. "That's a little extreme, don't you think. It would invite too much unwanted attention and if the police were very meticulous in their investigation, they might put two and two together. No, any such accident would need really careful planning and we just don't have enough time. I think the better idea would be to offer him a financial inducement to delay sending his report."

"What! You mean, bribe him?" Bill queried.

"Yes, even Ambassadors can be bought if the price is right." Craig would have been more certain about this belief if he knew about the gambling debts the Spanish Ambassador had incurred. Since moving to the United Kingdom Francisco Moran Aguirre regularly frequented the Capital's Casinos. He was not a lucky gambler but at first his losses were manageable. As he got more and more infected with the gambling fever his losses and debts dramatically increased. He had managed to hide this major draw on his personal finances from his wife and family, but the pressure on him to repay his debts was increasing. His only remedy would be to sell his home and most of his other assets, but even then the debt would still not be cleared. He had got himself into a real desperate situation and he couldn't see any way out of his horrible predicament.

"How much do you think it will take to get him to do what we want?" Bill asked.

"The financial rewards we stand to gain are enormous, while time is of the essence, so I think we need to make the bribe huge enough that he simply can't refuse."

"What sort of sum are you thinking about? Would five hundred thousand pounds swing it?" John asked.

Craig took a few minutes to think about the questions before giving his considered answer. He never rushed his decisions. His brain was like a computer programme that checked all the various permutations before choosing the best result. "Three million pounds," was the response. Both Bill and John Woodward couldn't believe what they had just heard. They were shocked. Even the haunting melody of Ennio Morricone's "Gabriel's Oboe", emanating from the Library, didn't help to reduce the now highly charged atmosphere.

"You must be joking!" John and Bill chorused in tandem after digesting the unexpected announcement.

"No, I'm deadly serious. This is chicken feed in relation to the hundreds of millions we stand to gain. We can't afford any slip-ups so this should ensure the Ambassadors co-operation."

"I can't imagine anyone, no matter how strong their principles are, refuse such a large amount of money," Bill said.

"I agree but the matter still has to be handled very delicately. As you have already met him, I want you to make contact and present the offer." *Is he really asking me to do this?* Bill thought to himself. Craig's odd coloured eyes seemed to have a silent language of their own, and the cold stare left Bill in no doubt that failure would not be tolerated.

"I'll make an appointment as soon as I return to London," Bill said knowing that he had no other option.

All the time that Bill was inside the magnificent Lochbuie Castle the helicopter pilot had been busy. He had supervised the refuelling of the helicopter. Some routine maintenance checks had also been carried out and Pete was satisfied that everything was in order for the return flight. Pete loved coming to Lochbuie with its outstanding natural beauty. After his pre-flight preparations were completed he managed to get some free time, to visit the well preserved stone circle overlooked by spectacular Ben Buie. As he enjoyed the scenery, he wondered why there was so much urgency in delivering the passenger with the withered left arm. He knew he was wasting his time with such thoughts, as there was a veil of secrecy covering everything to do with happenings at Lochbuie Castle. On returning to the helicopter he saw that his passenger was waiting for him.

"Pete, I've finished my business here and need to get back to London as soon as possible. Is everything ready for take-off?"

"Yes, the chopper is ready to go."

Chapter 25 – Bill's proposition

As Jim Wilson drew his bedroom curtains, he was greeted by bright sunshine streaming through and illuminating the room. On opening the window he felt a slightly chilly northwest wind, which would spoil an otherwise glorious start to another day. The temperature was about eleven degrees Celsius. From his viewpoint he could see beyond the harbour entrance, where the strengthening wind was pushing the white horses across the tops of the waves. Tom's experience told him that the presence of the white horses meant that the wind speed was about eleven to fifteen knots, registering four on the Beaufort scale. Not a perfect day, but it would be good enough to continue the search for *HMS Sussex*.

Jim had always kept himself very fit and over the years successfully competed in several marathons. He was really proud of the year in which he had entered both the London and New York Marathons, collecting over six thousand pounds in sponsorship for his favourite Cancer Charity. On checking his Rolex Deepsea Divers Watch he realised that there was enough time to take a five mile run, after competing his regular morning stretching exercises, and before returning to the support ship. Tom Dickson's villa was ideally located for anyone interested in jogging or running, as there were many suitable tracks and paths within a short distance from it. Jim had been really pleased when his colleague Gillian and he were invited to make Tom's villa their base whilst working on Project Sussex.

Gillian loved her bed. It always took a great deal of effort to get out of it each morning. There was to be no lie in for her this morning, however, as both she and Jim needed to return to the *MV Staffa*. She desperately hoped that today would be a day of discovery. The search area was quite large and she knew that it would not just take hard work, and constant vigilance, but a great deal of luck would also be needed. Today could be the day when the sea might reveal some clue to where their treasure ship was lying. If they were really, really lucky *HMS Sussex* herself might be found.

Not fully awake, she crept quietly down the hall stairs, so as not to disturb the others, and made her way to the kitchen. Not being an early morning person she urgently needed her "first fix" of hot, black, strong coffee, before she could face the challenges of the day. Jim had risen earlier and was already in the kitchen. "Going running?" Gillian mumbled through a huge yawn. She watched him fill his water bottle and place it into the fully insulated, angled bottle holster on his Nathan Triangle adjustable belt. Jim always had the proper gear and resources for whatever he was doing.

"Yes. Why don't you join me, it'll do you good?" Despite looking so pale and tired her beautiful brown eyes were as sexy as ever. Jim admired her very much, and in the short time they had know each other they had become good friends. There was no physical attraction between them but he still thought she had wonderful eyes.

"You must be joking. I don't do exercise, especially not at this time in the morning. You go, and I'll sit here and enjoy a cup of coffee."

"Ok, will do. See you later."

* * *

Any underwater hunt for treasure ships requires highly complex equipment, and relies on close teamwork to maximise the contribution from the multi-disciplined personnel involved. Jim Wilson was so grateful that the *MV Staffa* team were the best there was. If anybody could find the Sussex Gold then it would be them.

When Jim and Gillian arrived onboard the *MV Staffa* they found the two ROV Controllers carrying out pre-launch checks. All equipment onboard was the latest state-of-the-art design. Its ROV boasted a sophisticated positioning system, cameras and specialised computer hardware and software. Everything needed to be working perfectly, so great care was taken prior to any dive to conduct robotic operations thousands of feet below the Mediterranean. Once the checks were completed it didn't take long to have the ROV hoisted and swung overboard, by the ships crane, and then lowered into the water.

The main controller then remotely switched on the powerful hydraulic thrusters. Using his joystick he guided it down to its operational depth of a few meters above the sediment of the sea bed. Once in position Jim Wilson would be responsible for giving instructions to the ROV Controller, if he wanted to make any changes to the pre-planned grid pattern search. The second controller was responsible for operating the manipulator arms, which could lift objects comparable to the weight of an average man. He would also operate the Sediment Removal and Filtration System

Jim and Gillian took their positions in the Dive Control Centre. They wanted to ensure that all the necessary digital data being transmitted from the ROV was captured, and accurately processed on the ship's data logging system. Every second of the dive would be recorded on high-capacity digital video disk. The onboard systems also created a complete video and photo record which would be preserved indefinitely.

The first few hours passed uneventfully. Gillian was glued to one of the computer screens which showed video pictures of the seabed directly in front of the remotely controlled submersible. *This is boring*, she thought, although she didn't want to move away in case she missed something. "What? What's that?" Gillian moved closer to the computer screen to get a better view, in case her eyes were playing tricks on her. A tingling feeling of excitement coursed through her veins. "Jim, I think there's something there. Come and see."

Jim gave instructions for the ROV controller to hover near the spot identified by his colleague. Pulling up a chair next to Gillian, he sat down and stared at the screen. "It's not very clear but I think you're right."

Turning to the controller of the Sediment Removal and Filtration System he said, "Richard, can you use the Venturi hose to vacuum up some of the sediment surrounding and covering that dark brown object that you can see on your video monitor. Deposit the collected samples into the compartmentalized baskets, attached to the back of the ROV. When the dive is completed we'll have the samples sifted. When you're finished, use the hose to blow away the sediment covering the mystery object."

The occupants of the Dive Control Centre waited with bated breath as the sediment was slowly and gently cleared away from the protruding object. It was Richard who first recognised what it was. He couldn't believe what he was seeing. He was so happy and elated with the find.

He wanted to shout out loud. His throat had suddenly gone very dry and he could only manage a raspy squeak. "It looks like part of a ship's cannon."

* * *

Jim and Gillian were both unaware of the meeting that was currently taking place, over a thousand and sixty nine miles distant, in the capital of their home country. Soon after his return, from Lochbuie Castle, Bill Wyman contacted the Spanish Ambassador and arranged to meet with him. At first the Ambassador was reluctant to agree to the meeting as he had never met Bill Wyman. Bill was at his persuasive best and convinced him that it would be to his advantage. The Ambassador pressed for more details, but Bill simply told him that there were certain developments, concerning Project Sussex; he needed to be aware of.

"Good morning, Bill. Have a seat. Make yourself comfortable. Can I get you a drink?" Francisco Moran Aguirre disguised his reluctance for the meeting very well. He always worked to an Agenda and prepared accordingly. He didn't feel comfortable if he wasn't in full control. Just at this precise moment, he felt uncomfortable. "You told me you worked with Joshua Campbell, the British Minister for International Security Strategy although you didn't expand on your responsibilities. I know Joshua quite well but he has never spoken about you but nonetheless what can I do for you?" The mistake Francisco made was not checking with Joshua if Bill had been authorised to arrange this meeting. He would never fully understand why he hadn't followed his natural inclination to check on his visitor. He normally followed a policy of "No Surprises," and wanted to ensure that he wasn't caught "on the hop" with unexpected questions.

Bill refused the offer of a drink, but did choose to sit in the comfortable armchair directly opposite to the one now occupied by the Ambassador.

"I want you to refrain from sending any report to your Government, regarding Project Sussex."

The Ambassador was shocked by this totally unexpected forthright statement. He was far more used to the subtleties and nuances of diplomatic negotiations. He was often involved in verbal sparring bouts but this man, Bill possessed more of a pugilistic style. "I can't do that!!! It's my responsibility to keep my Government informed of any major matters, or events, which may have a direct affect on Spain. This Project is of tremendous importance and I must do my duty!"

Bill wanted to maintain the illusion that he had come to meet with the Ambassador, as a representative of the British Government. There was no need for him to know about Craig Burke or the real reason why Bill wanted to stop the report being sent. Bill waited for a few short minutes before replying to the Ambassadors angry retort. "We know about your huge gambling debts." Bill paused for a few seconds, to allow the Ambassador to absorb what he had said. "I am authorised to pay you three million pounds in return for your silence," Bill continued.

Chapter 26 – A Five Guinea Coin

It suddenly felt as if all the air had been completely sucked out of the room. He gasped for breath. His lungs were burning as he couldn't force enough oxygen to them. He was panic stricken. Fighting against the shock of what the man sitting opposite had said, the Ambassador slowly and gradually pulled himself together. *Was he dreaming or had he just been offered three million pounds?*

To become a successful career Diplomat takes a tremendous amount of hard work and dedication. Many personal sacrifices have to be made. It is essential to have excellent educational qualifications and come from a good background. Francisco Moran Aguirre possessed all the necessary attributes, skills and excellent family antecedents. His accomplishments were many, helping him climb up the ladder of success, the pinnacle of which was his appointment as Ambassador. Occasional visits to a casino to enjoy some Blackjack, the world's most widely played casino banking game in the world, gradually turned into an addiction. Before he got caught up in the tentacles of a huge gambling debt he did have some small wins, but they only helped fuel his compulsion. No one, not even his wife and close family, knew of this one major weakness, or at least that's what he believed until the staggering bribe was made.

At this precise moment he didn't feel successful, he felt weak and ashamed. He felt ashamed not only because his secret was no longer a secret, but ashamed because he had let both his family, and the country that he faithfully tried to serve, down.

"I don't have any gambling debts," he retorted. *What am I saying*, he thought as the words rushed from his mouth. He felt hot and cold, sick and sweaty with the revelation of his personal nightmare. Throughout his career he had always acted honourably, but was this temptation too much for him? He could settle all his gambling debts and still have a large sum of money left over. His family need never know how close they had come to financial ruin.

"Don't lie to me!" Bill Wyman snapped. "I've told you that we know. The ball's in your court. You haven't the cash resources to clear the debt, so you would be foolish not to accept this offer. Do I also need to remind you that the people you owe the money too can be very nasty, and would be prepared to harm you, and your family, if they don't get their money."

"They wouldn't harm my family!"

"Hurt your family? HA! Yeah, sure they are a family-orientated organisation. You are naive! They would stop at nothing to get their money."

What am I to do? Can I get away with this? I've never done anything dishonest before. Would they really harm my family? His head throbbed as he tried to sift through the numerous questions, and thoughts, which were bombarding him. Finally, he was ready. His mind was made up. Clasping his sweaty hands together he sat bolt upright. Looking directly at Bill Wyman, he took a deep breath and made his response.

"I accept," he whispered. His voice was shaky and almost inaudible.

"What did you say?"

"I'll do it!"

"Good. You won't regret this decision," Bill responded with a feeling of relief. "I'll be back in touch with you, in a few days, to agree how we will deal with the settlement of your debts. Don't get up, I'll see myself out."

When he was alone the stunned Ambassador poured himself a stiff drink as he tried to come to terms with what he had done.

As Bill made his way across London, to get back to his flat, he was glad that gambling wasn't one of his vices. He liked a flutter, once a year, when he had a day out at the Grand National meeting at Aintree Race Course. Last year he had favoured "Don't Push It" who was to be ridden by the thirty-five year old jump jockey, Tony McCoy. It was Tony's fifteenth attempt at this race but Bill had a good feeling about him, and placed a bet on him to win. Bill got odds of twenty-five to one and shortly after "Don't Push It" entered the winner's enclosure, he rushed to pick up his winnings of two and a half thousand pounds.

The first thing Bill did on arriving back at his flat was to contact Craig Burke at Lochbuie Castle. He needed to update him on the outcome of his meeting with the Spanish Ambassador. When he was last at Lochbuie Castle, Bill had been supplied with a new mobile telephone. Using this special mobile telephone service his calls could not be intercepted. Telephone companies keep records of telephone calls, including the number called, the calling number, and call data. His new secure mobile used an internet connection to transmit encrypted calls. He made the call safe in the knowledge that their communication would be in complete privacy.

"That's great news," Craig told Bill, after hearing about the Ambassador'. "Did he ask many questions about who was making the offer of such a large amount of money?"

"Not really, it went much easier than I expected. He thinks that I approached him on behalf of a British Government desperate to retrieve their gold. He hasn't a clue that I also work for you or about our plan to steal some of it. I think that deep down he was just so relieved to have the opportunity to clear his major gambling debt, and get out of the terrible mess he was in."

"Has Jack McDonald got his security team in place?"

"Yes, I heard from him recently and everything is going as planned. They arrived in Andalucía, onboard the *MV Staffa*, as scheduled. He's passed the letter of introduction to Tom Dickson as agreed." Bill replied. "Now that the Ambassador is effectively silenced I will contact Jack, again, and instruct him to move to the next stage of the operation."

"Keep in contact with this Francisco Moran Aguirre and make sure he doesn't have a change of heart. Let me know what plan you make with him to clear his debt, and I'll make the necessary arrangements." Having given his instructions Craig rang off.

* * *

The ROV controller hovered near to the dark brown object and carefully manoeuvred the Venturi hose to gently blow away the last of the sediment, which had covered it for over four hundred years. The powerful lights of the ROV penetrated the gloom, illuminating the scene sufficiently enough to allow the video cameras to do their work. A fairly clear image of an ancient ships cannon soon filled the monitor screen, at which Jim Wilson and Gillian Young were being mesmerised by the display.

"Could this be one of the eighty cannons which *HMS Sussex* carried?" Gillian asked.

"There is a high probability that it is. It's located near to the estimated site of the wreck. We'll need to widen the search and hopefully further evidence will be revealed. Once we get the ROV back on board we'll be able to sieve through the collected sediment samples." Jim replied.

"It's getting late now and I think we need to postpone our search until tomorrow." Gillian said rather reluctantly.

She felt that they had achieved a lot since commencing the search for the treasure ship. She possessed considerable vitality and seemed to have a limitless supply of energy. These qualities were invaluable and served to inspire the other team members. Even she however had to recognise that today's hunt was over.

"I agree," Jim said and then gave instructions to the ROV controller to bring it safely back to the mother ship.

As soon as the ROV was back on board, the sample sediment filled compartmentalised baskets were removed. Jim had already arranged for a three man specialist team to painstakingly sort through the sediment immediately as time was of the essence. This was a job that couldn't be hurried in case the tiniest piece of evidence was missed. He left them to their allocated task while he went to speak with Karl, the Captain of the *MV Staffa*. It was time to bring the Deep Rover Submersible and Dual Deep Worker into operation, but the permission of the Captain was needed before they could be launched.

It was important that the two submersibles dive together, as this added an additional safety factor. Jim had piloted a Deep Sea Rover on many occasions and was well used to its amazing high standard of performance. He was especially glad that no decompression procedure was required as the dive pressure inside the cabin remained at a constant one atmosphere.

"I'll pilot the Deep Sea Rover and take one of your crew as an observer. Gillian will remain on board in charge of the Dive Control Centre where I feel she will be most useful." Jim notified the Captain.

Before they could continue with their discussion they suddenly heard a loud, excited shout. Gillian was dashing towards them, "It's the *Sussex*!! It's the *Sussex*!!"

"Look at this Gold Coin," she could hardly get the words out quick enough as she thrust a coin into Jim's hand.

The coin had been found buried in the sediment which had been taken from the seabed. It had been cleaned and now shone a beautiful gold colour. The heads of the British King William III and Queen Mary appeared conjoined on this five guinea piece in Roman style, with William's head uppermost. The legend, GVLIELMVS ET MARIA DEI GRATIA, could also be clearly seen. The date marked on the coin was 1692, two years before the Sussex sunk.

Chapter 27 – Submersibles launched

Jack McDonald had never killed anyone in anger, but only when it was his duty. But today would not be a day for killing. Today would be uninteresting and frustratingly monotonous. No excitement, a day of following routine, dull and repetitive security checks. No security issues were identified; there would be nothing to get his teeth into. HE WOULD BE COMPLETELY BORED.

Ever since the *MV Staffa* had brought Jack McDonald and his security team to Andalucía, every day had been, more or less, the same. This state of low activity was something he wasn't used to. It hadn't always been like this, of course. When he served in the British SAS, life had been tremendously more adventurous and exciting. Many of his secret missions had been extremely hazardous, with his very life often being in jeopardy. Despite the risk he had loved every minute in the Special Air Forces, and was proud to hold the rank of Sergeant with this elite unit.
"A suicide car bomber blew up a small clinic in eastern Afghanistan on Saturday, causing the building to collapse as women and children waited in line. At least twenty people were killed in one of the deadliest attacks against civilians this year. It is also reported that at least thirty people have suffered horrific injuries," the CNN news reader announced as Jack drank his first strong coffee of the day. "Guards saw a sports utility vehicle charging toward the Akbarkhail Public medical Centre, a compound that provides health care for the mountainous area in the Azra district of Logar province. But before anyone could react the SUV smashed through a wall and exploded. Violence has been on the rise since the Taliban launched its spring offensive and promised retaliation for the death of Osama bin Laden."

As he watched this news broadcast on the small television, which was fixed to the wall of his cabin, his memory was stirred and he relived his most dangerous experience. He had led a small specialist team, not into Afghanistan, but to Iraq, another troubled Middle Eastern country. The mission purpose was to extract a senior diplomat who had been captured, and held hostage, by a very militant group of extremists. The negotiations stalled and were in danger of failing. If that happened the diplomat would no longer be of any value to his captors. As was the usual practice in such circumstances, the diplomat would suffer a cruel death by beheading. The executioners would make a video of this dreadful act and transmit it over the internet as sick propaganda. They would stop at nothing if it would further their unjustifiable cause. The location of where the diplomat was being held was disclosed by a trusted and reliable source. Time was running out, and so the decision was taken to send in Jack's well trained and disciplined team on a perilous rescue mission. It had been a bloody affair, as the SAS rescue team blasted their way into the villa, which was surrounded by Date Palms and other foliage. Despite a vicious and robust fire fight, the greater skill and experience of the SAS enabled them to kill all the militants, without their team suffering any fatalities. Sergeant Jack McDonald was so proud of the Military Cross he received for his bravery and gallantry in the leadership of his men.

Thank God, I'm finished for the day, Jack thought as he made his way back to the sanctuary of his cabin. His special secure mobile telephone buzzed. It was a text from his employer, Bill Wyman, *"All clear, progress plan."* The message was short and sweet but Jack knew exactly what to do. His first priority however, was to reach for the bottle of gin he had secreted in his cabin, for such a time of celebration. The frustrations of the day were soon forgotten as he poured himself a glass, topped it up with tonic, and placed a fresh wedge of Lime on the glass for garnish. His tired body was soon rejuvenated by the bitter sweet liquid.

Unknown to the captain and crew of the *MV Staffa*, Jack's men had carefully hidden four wooden boxes on board the support ship. The boxes contained various weapons. He would arrange for these to be discretely issued to the others in his team. His first task however was to get hold of a suitable used 18 Ton Box Truck with Tail Lift. He had made some provisional enquires and knew exactly where he could hire one. For a sizeable fee the supplier would store the vehicle until it was needed. For a further considerable fee he would falsify the necessary documentation so that the true hirer couldn't be traced. Jack had been instructed to steal some of the gold after it had been retrieved from the wreck, for which the Project Sussex Operational team were currently searching. How much he was to take would depend on the amount recovered, as the idea was not to let anyone become aware of the missing gold.

* * *

"It's not fair! You get all the exciting things to do. Why can't I be your observer on the Deep Rover Submersible?" Gillian complained.

"There is so much at stake here; therefore, I need someone in charge of the Dive Control Centre who is experienced and reliable. As far as I am concerned you are the best person to do this, and would be of more use than just sitting beside me as my observer."

"You're just trying to flatter me so that I won't feel so upset."

"No, I really mean it; I trust you implicitly and need to know that when the Deep Rover is beneath the waves a highly competent person is in control of the overall operation."

"Ok, fine! I'll do as you want!" Gillian succumbed rather ungraciously; she really wanted to be close to the wreck should it be discovered.

Following the pre-dive briefing, onboard the mother ship, the twin Deep Rover and Dual Worker submersibles were launched. Their compact size and relatively small tonnage made the launch process fairly easy, especially in average to moderate sea conditions. Leaning over the deck rail Gillian and the ship's captain watched the submersibles, as they bobbed about with a slight swell on the beautifully blue waters of the Mediterranean. Jim Wilson had already taken his place on the Deep Rover. He was really impressed by the updated and safer means of access. Flooding used to be a major risk especially when the submersible was on the surface. If the access hatch was opened prematurely it allowed water to enter the pressure hull. The new configuration with a bottom hatch eliminated this problem.

"These submersibles look so futuristic that they wouldn't look out of place in a science fiction film," Gillian remarked to her companion.

As there was no response, Gillian turned to look directly at him. She saw he had become quite agitated, trying to attract the attention of the submersibles crews. "LOOK OUT! LOOK OUT! THE SWELL IS BRINGING THE SUBMERSIBLES TOGETHER!"

The warning was unnecessary, as the pilots were already aware of the danger. Their speedy corrective action prevented damage to the manipulator arms, or the 3,000 metre depth rated externally fitted digital camera.

Seated in the comfortable cabin of the Deep Rover Jim Wilson peered through the acrylic observation sphere. Spotting Gillian on the deck of the *MV Staffa*, he gave her the "Thumbs Up." The sphere would allow him an unparalleled 320 degree field of view. He was really happy about this dive opportunity; he knew it would be a magical experience. He had no worries about the reliability and safety of his vehicle, for it had been well tested with over two hundred previous dives to its credit. Both the Deep Rover and Deep Worker Submersibles possessed the latest up-to-date communication systems. Communications between the two pressure hulls was achieved with the internal PA system. Once subsea he would use the Newtcom single frequency 27KHz digital underwater telephone, to maintain contact with the support ships Dive Control Centre. When the submersibles were on the surface, a standard marine VHF radio would be used.

Both Jim and Gillian had confidence in their plan for the dive. They had spent hours discussing the various options and resources required. Being an extremely versatile piece of kit, the ROV had been chosen to lead the search. It accommodated a range of state of the art sensors, together with an assortment of other specialist equipment. Its versatility would enable it to get extremely close to the seabed, where its powerful LED lights, and strong flexible manipulator arms, could be most efficiently used.

Driven by its four powerful thrusters the Deep Rover would follow in support. This would allow various additional features to be brought into play, such as the Simrad MS900 colour imaging sonar system. The two six function, rate-controlled, Hawke sensory manipulators would also be very valuable.

If and when the wreck was found, the Deep Rover would then place undersea acoustic beacons around the dive site, enabling further navigation to be precise at all times. The Dual Deep Worker would add further flexibility to the operation. It was unable to go as deep as the Deep Rover, but would provide an additional lighting platform. *Yes, it was a good plan.* There was no time left to dwell on the plan. All his attention was needed to pilot the Deep Rover as it slowly submerged beneath the waves.

The *Servicio Maritime de la Guardia Civil* is the Spanish Customs and border protection agency, which operates a fleet of sixty-seven patrol vessels and speedboats. Jim Wilson would not have been so confident with his plans, if he knew that one of these patrol boats, with the bright red hull and superstructure, was churning up what looked like a line of whipped cream in its wake, as it headed directly for the *MV Staffa*.

Chapter 28 – Target discovered?

Any student of Spanish history would know about Manuel de Montiano, the Governor of La Florida, who was involved in the Battle of Jenkins' Ear. Tensions between Great Britain and Spain had been on the rise for years, and on October 30, 1739 Great Britain declared war on Spain. The War of Jenkins' Ear was fought as part of a larger conflict, the War of Austrian Succession. The name comes from an incident involving one Robert Jenkins. Jenkins was the captain of the brig *Rebecca* in 1731. By the Treaty of Seville, Britain was barred from trading with Spain's colonies in the new world. However, smugglers could make a nice profit if they managed to avoid the Spanish coast guard. Jenkins wasn't a good enough captain to avoid them, so his ship was boarded by the Spanish coast guard La Isabela and he was punished by having his ear cut off. The Manuel de Montiano, who captained the Spanish coastguard vessel bearing down on the *MV Staffa*, wasn't a descendent of the Spanish Governor; he simply shared the same name.

It was almost a year since Manuel had been part of the team that had intercepted the Destiny Princess, in rough waters two hundred miles off the coast of Galicia. Forty bales of high-grade cocaine weighing about 1.5 tonnes had been discovered in a hidden compartment of the ship, accessed through a bolted trap door under a carpet. British police said the shipment would have been worth £375 million on the streets. Although he was only twenty-nine years of age successful participation in such seizures had helped to fast track him to his present command.

The *Solana* was named after Francisco Javier Solana de Madariaga, a famous Spanish physicist and Socialist politician. After serving in the Spanish Government he became the Secretary General of NATO.

Following this appointment he went on to undertake many European Union appointments, including becoming the Secretary General of the Council of the European Union. Manuel was very proud to be in command of such a fine and well named vessel.

Manuel was not a politician, nor did he ever aspire to be one. But he was grateful to have been given the responsibility of being in charge of this latest addition to the Spanish Coastguard's fleet. An ambitious man, he was always on the lookout for opportunities to advance his career. He didn't hesitate therefore, to deviate from his planned course when the hive of activity around the *MV Staffa*, was spotted. Manuel held back from reporting his unscheduled investigation, for if he discovered anything untoward he would gain much credit, and perhaps even further promotion. Looking through his powerful binoculars, the name of the target ship could be clearly read. Lowering his binoculars, and turning to his radio operator he said, "Contact the *Staffa*, and inform them to prepare to receive some visitors."

* * *

The Captain of the *MV Staffa* had just left the Bridge, leaving his First Officer in command. Karl both liked and completely trusted his young second-in-command. Over the six years they had served together, a strong bond of friendship had developed between them as they shared in many exciting adventures. Robert, the First Officer originated from Dublin, in the Republic of Ireland, he lived up to the general view of what typified an Irishman. He had red hair, freckles, enjoyed Irish dancing in his spare time, and was blessed with the "gift of the gab." People with red hair are often considered as having a fiery temperament, but this wasn't the case with the First Officer of the *MV Staffa*. Generally he was very calm and not prone to panic, although there was a touch of excitement in his voice when he broadcasted over the ships tannoy system, "Captain to the Bridge! Captain to the Bridge!"

As he hadn't got very far, it took only a few minutes for the Captain to return, "What's up? I need to get ready to meet our Spanish Visitors."

"Sir, I don't think you'll need to bother. The *Solana* is changing track and pulling away."

"Have they let us know what they're up to?"

"No, Sir, no radio messages have been received."

"Try and get through to them," the captain ordered.

After a few minutes of trying to raise the *Solana*, on their Marine VHF Radio, the First Officer replaced the transmitter in its holder as there was no response. No one onboard the *MV Staffa* would ever discover why the coast guard patrol boat had changed course.

Manuel de Montiano brought his officers together. "We are to join a special NATO Rescue Mission, which is being formed to help the boat people who are trying to escape from the Libyan civil war. It seems four hundred people were rescued recently after their boat smashed against rocks in the Mediterranean. The steering failed and the boat foundered in strong winds off the Italian island of Lampedusa."

"Isn't that section of the Mediterranean outside our area of jurisdiction?" one of the officers asked.

"Yes, under normal circumstances it is, but the Italians are under resourced and have asked for help from other NATO countries. A concentrated effort needs to be made in order to save lives. People are being killed if they remain in Libya; the least we can do is make every effort to save them from dying at sea. I've asked the navigator to plot a new course, so gentlemen, let's set about our duties and get to our allotted station as quickly as possible."

* * *

As he piloted the Deep Rover deeper beneath the surface of the water, Jim Wilson grinned from ear to ear. No matter how many dives he completed, he never took this privilege for granted. "This is great! I get goose pimples every time I make a dive like this. I love every minute of it," he said to his Observer.

It was a well known fact that the waters off the coast of Andalucía are home to a large population of whales and dolphins. He couldn't believe his luck, when earlier in the day as preparations for the dive were made; a Baleen whale was spotted off the bow of the support ship. Jim had seen many porpoise and dolphins over the years but never such a magnificent creature as this Baleen, which appeared to be as large as a Boeing B-747.

Just under the Mediterranean waves there was a whole world waiting to be explored. Jim knew that large numbers of people, snorkelling on the surface of the water, would be enjoying the experience of a limited exploration. His work provided him with the greater opportunity to experience a much more varied marine life. Dive sites provide a mix of rocky underwater landscapes, reefs and wrecks. The waters around Gibraltar especially, have a number of interesting wrecks, although none were as interesting as the reason for his current adventure to try and find HMS Sussex. In terms of marine life, congers, groupers, seahorses, spider crabs, squid, lobster, trigger fish, sunfish and dolphins were plentiful.

The search was recommenced from the spot where the five guinea gold coin and cannon were found. Gillian was able to follow the operation from her position in the support vessel's Dive Control Centre. The pictures, being received from the ROV and Deep Rover, were creating quite a stir as they were displayed on the computer monitors. Further evidence, of the existence of HMS Sussex, was taking form on the screens. Various objects and nautical artefacts were seen lying on the seabed. Turning to the ROV controller she said, "Move the ROV further to the right and bring it closer to the seabed. I think those objects are from a ship but we need to illuminate them better to get a clearer view."

"Is that any better?" the controller responded as he manipulated the controls to reposition the ROV.

"Its better but the images are still not clear enough. The Deep Rover has been fitted with side scanners and their imaging sonar can transform the things we cannot see underwater into pictures of near photographic quality, in any visibility." Picking up the transmitter of the Newtcom underwater telephone Gillian contacted the Deep Rover.

"Jim, we are receiving some good images from the video cameras but I think we need extra help from the imaging sonar. Can you bring them into action?"

"Ok, will do." Choosing the appropriate switch from the array in front of him, he reported back to Gillian, "The side scanners are now live."

Inside the acrylic sphere Jim manipulated the joystick, controlling the four five horsepower thrusters, to guide the Deep Rover forward into a new section of the search grid. He could see that the ROV was also altering course and being pushed slightly ahead of his craft. He knew that the Deep Worker would still be maintaining its position overhead. Two hours had now elapsed and although some indication that a wreck, possibly the *Sussex*, could be near, no actual sighting had been made.

"Can you see them?" Jim questioned his Observer.

"Yes, I count six barnacle encrusted cannon."

The cannon were partly covered by the soft mud and sediment of the seabed, but the protruding tops of the encrusted cannons were visible to the keen eyesight of Jim and his companion.

"Let's get closer. I'll get Gillian to move the ROV and focus its powerful lights onto the cannons."

As Jim finished speaking, and before he could contact her, he heard Gillian's voice in his headset. "Jim, the side scanners have picked up very clear images of a wreck beneath the seafloor. It appears to fit the description of the *Sussex*. On the monitors we can also see that a large number of boxes have been thrown clear of the wreck. They could easily be the type of container that was used to carry gold coins."

Chapter 29 – Spanish intervention

"It's nearly four hours since we started this dive, so we've only got another four hours before the submersibles have to be recovered. Let's get the ROV working in conjunction with the Deep Rover, to maximise the time left. Use the Venturi hose again and clear the muck from the large chests." Gillian said to the ROV controller.

As the powerful hose "dusted off" the large boxes, in which it was hoped a rich cargo of gold coins would be found, dark clouds of sediment were swirled around the containers hiding most of them. "I can only make out three," the ROV controller said as he watched the flickering images on his monitor in the cramped control room.

"Three, is enough for us to be getting on with. Once the sediment settles move the ROV in closer. The robotic arms are strong enough to lift the boxes, one at a time, if they can get a good grip of something solid and unmoveable. Test that protuberance encircling the container, if you're not satisfied that it'll hold, we'll need to put chains on it."

The ROV controller was very experienced and had coped with many similar delicate operations. He knew steady hands were needed to manipulate the joystick. He knew that every time it was moved, a computer sent an electronic signal to one of the instruments which operated the jaws of the grippers. He knew he could do it.

"Great, you've got it moving. Once you pull it free from the clutch of the seafloor bring it to the Deep Worker and place it on its platform. In the meantime, I'll get Jim to use the Deep Rover's Hawke sensory manipulators to salvage another container," Gillian continued.

Unknown to the occupants of the Dive Control Centre who were so engrossed with their various duties, Jack McDonald, the leader of the security team, had come in. He had never seen so much activity in such a small room. The data-loggers, were systematically documenting some of the large volume of information being captured by the on-board computers. Other technicians were busy doing technical things. The ROV controller was busy controlling. Gillian loved the buzz she always got from co-ordinating all the various activities.

Jack was not a computer person in any shape or form, but he was fascinated with the amazing images he could see on the monitor's that the technicians were glued too. They seemed to be speaking in a foreign language as they used much technical jargon, but there was no mistaking the evidence of the large container being carried through the depths, by the ROV.

* * *

"World's most expensive men's bespoke suit on sale for £600,000." The headline drew Bill Wyman's attention to the front page story in his morning paper. As he drank his Americano he read on. It was reported that this "ultimate in luxury fashion" had been encrusted with diamonds and would make any man stand out from the crowd. *I think it should. Some people must have more money than sense.* Bill always had his own suits made to measure. His withered left arm made it difficult for him to purchase "off the peg" suits which would fit him properly. Although his suits were expensive he would never ever contemplate paying such an extortionate sum of money. As he didn't possess the wealth to support such a lavish lifestyle, such expenditure could never become a reality. Putting his paper down he allowed his mind to drift. *I will be able to acquire whatever I want with my share of the gold. Suits, cars, property, investments, travel, private aeroplane, yachts—whatever I want.* The ringing of his mobile brought him back to reality. He knew from the caller identification that he was about to receive important information.

"Yes, Jack."

His heart beat faster. His grip tightened on his mobile phone. He was completely riveted. He was ecstatic. Pressing the phone tighter to his ear ensured he didn't miss anything. "They've actually located the ship and are starting to retrieve chests from the sea floor?" he stuttered into the mouthpiece.

"I've been watching the images from the submersibles and I've seen everything I've told you, with my own eyes."

"That's great news. Have you got everything in place?"

"Yeah, all sorted. We can move as soon as you give the order."

They wouldn't have been so euphoric if they knew that the two diesel engines of a Spanish Offshore Patrol Vessel were propelling it towards the *MV Staffa*. Manuel de Montiano had changed his mind. As the *Solana* progressed on its humanitarian mission, he reconsidered his decision not to report the activities of the *MV Staffa*. *I can benefit here. Report my suspicions. Succeed with helping the Libyan refugees, double benefit.* Summoning his radio operator he said, "Juan, I need you to send an urgent message to headquarters." This message had spurred the Spanish authorities into acting with unbelievable speed resulting in the despatch of the *Meteoro*.

This vessel, recently launched and put into service, was a high performance mission versatility ship. It was used to control maritime traffic and to control fishing laws. It operated against piracy and terrorism amongst many other important roles. Now its job was to prevent any further unauthorised activities. The Spanish ship had a crew of thirty five personnel and a forces compliment of the same number, six of whom were transferred on board the *MV Staffa* to take it under Spanish control.

The tone of Jack's voice suddenly changed on realising that something was happening on deck. There seemed to be a sense of panic spreading through the ship. He could hear shouting but couldn't hear what was being said. "Bill, I need to go. Something's happening on deck. I'll phone you back when I know what's going on." He had become very agitated. Cutting the call abruptly, he ran to find the source of the commotion.

Before this sudden interruption Bill had decided to inform both the British Defence Minister, as well as his criminal associate, Craig Burke, the good news of the find when the call was ended. In the light of this latest development, he thought it more prudent to hold off until Jack got back to him. *I hope nothing serious is happening? Could the project be at risk? Pull yourself together man, it's probably nothing. I need something stronger than an Americano.* Failure wasn't an option for Bill. He had an inbuilt belief that he could always make his own destiny no matter who got hurt on the way. Twenty four hours later his firmly held belief would be rocked to the core.

* * *

It was still dark when James Martindale left his home in Kilmacolm. It was only a short drive to his office at AB Salvage, in Greenock, but he had a board meeting to prepare for, and wanted to get there before the other directors arrived. As Managing Director he had steered the company through several recessions together with an increasing number of competitive threats. He loved a challenge and had great vision. His inspired leadership allowed his other board members to make their own significant contributions to the growth of the company.

He had made himself a brew before settling down to get his papers in order when he was disturbed by the ringing of his phone. It was a call he wasn't expecting and certainly it was news he didn't want to hear. The Captain of the *MV Staffa* only contacted him when there was something important to report. "Karl, you have no option but to do as they want. I'll contact Bill Wyman to let him know this disastrous news. He can contact everybody that needs to know that Project Sussex has been halted, that's if they don't know already. Just you make sure that you don't do anything to put the ship in jeopardy with the Spanish Authorities. Is Jim Wilson and Gillian alright?"

"Jim and Gillian are Ok except that they're obviously devastated that they can't continue the project. They, like me, are also so frustrated. The Spanish are not giving any reasons for their actions. The only thing we know is that the *MV Staffa* is to move to one of their naval bases. They've also hit a brick wall in trying to find out when we can recommence the project."

"Tell them to be patient I'm sure that it will soon get sorted. Where are they escorting you too?"

"I've been ordered to make course for the naval base at Rota, near to the Spanish town of El Puerto de Santa Maria."

"Karl, I need to move quickly and report this terrible situation. I'll get back to you as soon as I can."

Once he put his phone down James took a few moments o gather his thoughts, in the quietness of his office. This was very bad news. Everything had been going so well and now the Spanish Authorities have prevented further progress. Picking up his phone he dialled the number. The connection was made within seconds. "Bill, we have a problem."

* * *

The upper echelons of the British Government were rampant with activity, following the appalling news regarding the intervention by the Spanish. The Defence Minister had received a copy of the Spanish Despatch, from his fellow Cabinet Minister at the Foreign Office. He had also heard "first hand" from Bill Wyman. "William, you need to use every diplomatic means at your disposal, to find out what's going on. We need to get this project back on track; there's too much at stake to have any further delays. Billions of pounds could be lost."

"You don't need to remind me, I know the situation and have already put matters in hand," the Foreign Secretary replied. He was annoyed with the insinuation that he was not aware of the seriousness of the circumstances. From the tone of the original notification, he sensed that it would probably be many years before there was any hope of recommencing the dive.

Bill Wyman had thought it wise to notify the Defence Minister as soon as he knew the circumstances. He wished to keep close contact and didn't want to get sidelined. He wasn't so keen to get in touch with his criminal master. Craig Burke would be furious and would see this as a sign of failure. He wasn't a reasonable man and wouldn't listen to excuses.

"Did any of the chests contain gold? Did the dive team manage to get any of the chests onboard the *MV Staffa*? How did they find out about the project? Is there a traitor in our midst?" Craig interrogated.

Bill could only answer "I don't know," to each of the barbed questions that were being thrown at him down the earpiece of the phone.

In an attempt to deflect Craig's anger from himself he said, "Perhaps the Spanish Ambassador . . . ."

Before he could finish, Craig interrupted him, "He was paid three million pounds to keep quite! Are you telling me he took the money but didn't keep his end of the bargain?" Craig's knuckles were pure white as he gripped the phone even tighter wishing it was Bill Wyman's neck. He was so angry that he could feel his heart racing in his chest, the blood pulsing hot and fast through his veins. Unaware that Manuel de Montiano had changed his mind, or that it was he who had reported the activities of the *MV Staffa*, Craig told Bill to report any developments and then slammed the phone down.

* * *

Francisco Moran Aguirre always had a shower, each morning, before setting off for his Embassy. The warmth of the water cascading over his back was quite welcoming. He enjoyed being blanketed by the water, enjoying every moment of its warm wet blanket. As he got lost in thought, he lathered up his body, almost by second nature. He couldn't believe his good fortune, all his financial problems and worries had been solved at a stroke. He didn't have to commit a robbery. He didn't have to commit murder. All he had to do was not file a report and he was three million pounds the richer.

Getting dressed quickly, he had a light breakfast. He felt that he could cope better with the issues of the day if he didn't have too much to eat in the morning. As he wanted to try out his new Mercedes SL Series with the Vario-Roof, which could transform the hardtop coupe to an open top roadster in only sixteen seconds, he wasn't going to use his official car.

Throwing his briefcase onto the brown leather passenger seat, Francisco eased himself into the driving position. Inserting his key into the ignition he turned it on. The Spanish Ambassador never heard the thump of the explosion as the force of the blast ripped through his car. He was killed outright. Body and car parts were scattered all over the road. The fuel tank had been torn apart spraying its contents all over the vehicle. The intense heat from the explosion set the fuel on fire and the remains of the car were being cremated. At that early hour of the morning traffic was very light, and as a consequence there were no other casualties.

The dark haired man, who had been watching the carnage from a flat, some five hundred yards across the small square, drew the curtains, picked up his secure mobile telephone, dialled Craig Burke's number and sent a text, *INFORMER DEAD.*

Lightning Source UK Ltd.
Milton Keynes UK
UKOW050915211011

180696UK00002B/14/P